"Don't turn into a weeping Niobe."

Gray Crawford's words were chiding. "Brave women send their men into battle with smiles."

And so she smiled until her lips were stiff, all through breakfast and during their goodbyes. Gray's final embrace was perfunctory as he said lightly, "When I come back I'll crown you with my victor's laurels."

Frances watched his car disappear into the gray murk with a sense of foreboding. Suppose, among the bevy of American fans, he came to regret his hasty marriage to her? Gray was the love of her life, but her hold on him was so slight!

It was time to return to Craig Dhu. In the car Frances surreptitiously slipped off her wedding ring. She was Miss Desmond again—until Gray came back to claim her.

ELIZABETH ASHTON
is also the author of these
Harlequin Romances

and this
Harlequin Presents

Silver Arrow

by

ELIZABETH ASHTON

Harlequin Books

TORONTO • LONDON • LOS ANGELES • AMSTERDAM
SYDNEY • HAMBURG • PARIS • STOCKHOLM • ATHENS • TOKYO

Original hardcover edition published in 1980
by Mills & Boon Limited

ISBN 0-373-02425-8

Harlequin edition published September 1981

CHAPTER ONE

THE speedboat went by like a hurricane, suddenly appearing behind the launch and vanishing up the loch ahead of it. Frances Desmond caught a glimpse of white bows high above the water and a cloud of spray, The wake from its passage whipped the sea into a miniature whirlpool rocking the slower craft.

'Speedhog!' she exclaimed indignantly, clutching at the side of the boat as it rose and fell. She was tired after her long journey to the Western Highlands and apprehensive about her welcome at her destination, so that the speedboat's incivility seemed a menace. Although she had been warned about it when she accepted the post she had not realised that Craig Dhu was so remote and could only be reached by water. She had been met at Mallaig by the young man who was manipulating the controls, Ian Ferguson, her new employer's son, and he had explained that though there was a rough track over the mountains, they always used the boats for transport.

Ian laughed as the waves of wash receded and the motor launch regained its equilibrium.

'That was Gray Crawford in Silver Arrow,' he told her, and as she wrinkled her brows. 'Surely you've heard of Graham Crawford?'

She shook her dark head and he stared at her.

'Where have you been vegetating?' he demanded. 'Perhaps ...' his tone became sarcastic, 'you've never heard of Sir Malcolm Campbell?'

'Yes, of course, I'm not that ignorant, but I thought he was a motor racer.'

'Water as well. He held the record in 1939, but his son beat it in '59. Silver Arrow makes him look like a tortoise.'

'So this Mr Crawford is a speed ace?'

'Just about top notch.' The young man's face was alight with hero-worship. 'Didn't Mother mention him when she wrote to you?—No, I suppose she wouldn't. We rent Craig Dhu from the Crawfords, and Gray lodges here when he's testing boats on the loch. I and Lesley, that's my sister, service them.'

'Mrs Ferguson did mention her son and daughter.' Frances looked about her. They had left the open sea and somewhat grim-looking hills rose on either side of them. Behind them the sunset flared over the Western Isles, the sharp points of the Cuillins identifying Skye; although it cast a golden glow over water and hills, the scene was still a little forbidding. On a dull day it would look sombre. 'Isn't this a very isolated spot for an invalid lady?'

'Oh, my mother isn't really an invalid,' Ian told her. 'To be frank it's a bit of a pose to draw attention to herself, for I'm afraid my sister and I are apt to become absorbed in our own concerns. She must have told you she's a widow. But you won't find her exacting,' he added hastily, for it had not been easy to engage a help who was willing to come to such a desolate spot. 'You were warned we were very cut off.'

'I don't mind that,' Frances assured him, for she had been as anxious to obtain the job as the Fergusons had been to employ her. Since she had left school she had lived at home with her parents, as she was the only child of a middle-aged couple, and while her father was alive had had an adequate social life, though her mother, being selfish and delicate, had made considerable demands upon her. After he died, their income dwindled and her mother became more demanding, as she developed leukaemia. When she succumbed to it, Frances found herself left with a small inheritance and a need to find a paid occupation to augment it. Trained for nothing and without experience, a domestic post seemed her only hope and the Fergusons offered a generous salary, though the prospect of assisting with another ailing woman was not inspiring, but at least she knew all about that.

'It seems very fine country,' she went on to placate him.

'You haven't visited the Highlands before?'

'No, I've never been to Scotland.'

'To my mind there's no place on earth as lovely as this country,' he told her earnestly. 'I hope you'll learn to love it too.'

His dark eyes were assessing her with open admiration. The girl was not at all what he had expected. He had envisaged a country wench, fair, fresh-faced, possibly a little heavy since she came from rural Kent, but Frances had a matt white skin and hair like black silk. Her eyes, under level black brows, were blue, nearly violet, with a dreamy, almost fey expression that he had hitherto associated with women of his own race, but with her colouring she might be a Celt. Her name was Irish, and he asked if that were so, but she denied it.

'I might have Irish ancestors, but my family have always lived in south-east England.'

She felt a wave of homesickness for the pretty countryside she had left. There was something vaguely menacing about these gaunt hills; then she shook herself mentally. She was tired and that made her fanciful. The young man escorting her seemed normal and friendly; dark-haired, dark-eyed, he had the rangy build of the Highlander. He would look well in a kilt, she thought, but there was nothing especially Scottish about him; except for a faint roll of the rs, his speech was anglicised. If the rest of the family were like him she need not be apprehensive.

They rounded a bend in the loch and he pointed ahead.

'Craig Dhu.'

The house was on a promontory extending into the loch. It stood high on a rocky eminence, and sheltering behind it on the landward side was a natural harbour, with a stone jetty. It was an old Scottish castle, the original tower rising stark above the water, but it had been modernised and built on to. Trees and shrubs grew on its eastern sheltered side, that towards the sea was bare and grim.

'Looks a bit formidable from here,' Ian remarked, 'but I assure you it's quite comfortable inside and we have all mod cons.'

He guided the motor launch round the bluff into the cove where several boats of various sorts rode at anchor and there were sheds and workshops built along the shore.

'We often have craft up here for trial runs during

the summer,' Ian told her. 'Crawfords' works are at Glasgow, they're boatbuilders, you know.'

Frances had not known, Mrs Ferguson had not mentioned the Crawfords.

Ian shut off the engine and the launch glided into the jetty. A man was standing on it, talking to a girl. Both wore wet suits, close-fitting as skins, the man's being black, the girl's red. There was something a little diabolical about their appearance and to Frances' excited imagination they only needed tails to pose as demonic imps, and both had a sinuous feline grace. The girl's head was bare, she had a small, catlike face, disfigured by an oily streak across her nose, and a bush of thick brown hair; the man wore a hood and goggles. As the boat's fender touched the quay he made an impatient gesture and strode away, but the girl came running to catch the rope Ian threw towards her and secure it to a mooring ring.

'Something wrong?' Ian asked anxiously, as the girl extended a not very clean hand to assist the newcomer on to the jetty.

'Oil leak trouble, a job for us to locate it.'

The girl had a deep voice at variance with her slight figure and small face. She had wide-spaced greenish eyes and a pointed chin.

'Seemed going all right as she came up the loch,' Ian observed. Then he remembered his passenger. 'My sister Lesley,' he said to Frances.

Lesley Ferguson detached her mind from engine trouble and favoured the new help with a long critical stare.

'Gray didn't stay to be introduced,' Ian went on.

So the black devil was the speed ace, Frances grasped, just landed from the silver bomb that had flashed up the loch and far too immersed in technical problems to stay to greet a stranger—a conjecture Lesley bore out as she said:

'He'd other things on his mind. Good God, girl, how young you are! Miss . . . er . . . Desmond, isn't it?'

'Yes, and I'm twenty-three,' Frances returned stiffly, annoyed by the girl's exclamation and her insolent manner.

'You'll never stick this place,' Lesley told her. She prided herself upon being brutally frank.

'Girls of your age expect entertainment, shops, and . . .' her eyes narrowed '. . : young men. There's nothing like that here.'

'There's me,' Ian pointed out, as he put Frances' cases on the jetty, 'and Frances was warned about the lack of amusements.'

'Frances?' Lesley raised thin arched brows.

'She's to be like one of the family, I'm not going to Miss Desmond her,' Ian declared.

Lesley looked down her short nose. 'The home help?' she sneered.

'Exactly, we want to make her feel at home, don't we?'

'So long as she doesn't forget to help. Come along, Miss Desmond,' she emphasised the name. 'My brother will bring your gear. My mother is anxious to meet you.'

She led the way along the jetty and up a steep path to the entrance to the house. Frances followed, wondering why the girl seemed so antagonistic, since it was obvious she was not being welcomed by Miss Ferguson. Ian followed them carrying her cases, his brows puckered. He was perturbed by his sister's attitude. She had applauded the idea of obtaining help in the house, but she should be more friendly if she wanted to keep it. A small community in such isolation were totally dependent upon each other and needed a harmonious relationship.

'When you've taken Miss Desmond's luggage up, you'd better get back to the sheds,' Lesley told her brother. 'I'll join you later. That engine will have to be overhauled.' She glanced at Frances. 'I'm an engineer,' she announced with pride.

'Oh, are you?'

That accounted for her garb and the oily streak across her nose. Frances knew women were invading the hitherto masculine trades, but she was surprised to be given definite proof of it. Lesley looked too slight and delicately made to handle spanners, bolts and nuts, but possibly such work required more knack than strength.

They reached an imposing iron-studded oak door and Lesley pushed it open as a large dog bounded towards them, a Great Dane, as big as a calf, who eyed the stranger doubtfully.

'You like dogs?' Lesley enquired disdainfully.

'Yes.' Frances held out a tentative hand. She was not afraid of any animal, though this one looked intimidating.

The dog sniffed it cautiously, then began to wag his tail.

'Good, Caesar has accepted you,' said Ian as Frances stroked the massive head.

Lesley made no comment, though her expression was eloquent. She would have been better pleased if Caesar had growled at her.

The door gave access to a huge stone paved hall with a wide staircase of polished oak, ascending to the upper regions. There was a large open fireplace stacked with logs, but not alight, and although it was early summer the place felt damp and chill. An oaken settle was against one wall and a row of pegs carrying outdoor clothing along another. An array of rubber boots were in one corner, a lifebelt and boat gear in another, for the great hall at Craig Dhu was used for utilitarian purposes. There were several doors, and Lesley opened one of them while Ian proceeded upstairs with Frances' cases.

'My mother is in here.'

A few feet of stone passage and another door, and they stepped through into the more modern part of the house. Lit by electric light—it was Scotland's boast that however remote the region electricity was always available—as the long northern twilight gave insufficient illumination, Frances saw a big low-ceilinged room, comfortably furnished with deep armchairs, a sofa, thick carpet and velvet curtains at the windows overlooking the loch. A women reclined on the sofa with a rug over her feet, and a table beside her littered with magazines and an empty coffee cup. A small wood fire burned in the grate. Margaret Ferguson had small features surrounded by soft brown hair streaked with grey, her eyes, like her son's, were dark. She looked delicate and held out a languid hand to the newcomer.

'Miss Desmond,' Lesley said succinctly.

'Welcome to Craig Dhu,' Margaret greeted Frances in a low die-away voice. 'I hope you'll be happy here, but it's a bit of a mausoleum.' She looked at her daughter. 'Ask Morag to bring some tea, will you, dear? It's still some time until supper, and I'm sure Miss Desmond would like some. Sit by me, Miss Desmond, and I'll explain your duties to you.' She indicated the end of the sofa by her feet, and her gaze returned to her daughter, frowning as she noticed her appearance. 'Couldn't you have washed before our visitor arrived?'

'She's not a visitor,' Lesley pointed out. 'She's a help, and I'm working in the sheds. I can't keep spick and span when I'm busy. I'll tell Morag about the tea and then Miss Desmond had better see her room, and perhaps she'll lend a hand with supper.'

She stalked out of the room and her mother watched her go with a troubled expression.

'I can't get used to girls doing men's work,' she sighed. 'Les is always covered in oil and looks so unglamorous. How she can expect to attract Gray looking like that, I can't imagine.' She brightened. 'Though they do have a kindred interest in Silver Arrow.'

Thus unconsciously she betrayed her daughter's secret, and Frances guessed the reason for Lesley's antagonism. She had been dismayed to find the new help was young and not ill-favoured, fearing she might be a rival for the speed merchant's favours. Possibly Gray Crawford was not only fast with boats. She need have no qualms, Frances thought bitterly; she was immune to masculine charms, after the defection of Tony Archer. She had believed he was her friend and their association dating from teen-age years would ripen into a closer relationship, but as her mother's health declined and her expectations faded, so had his affection shrunk. When she was left almost destitute, Tony lost interest, and at a time when she needed his support most. It was another reason for accepting this far-distant post. Her Kentish friends and neighbours had expected him to marry her and she had wilted under their pitying looks. Her vanity more than her heart was hurt—the latter, although she did not realise it, had been hardly touched—but she mourned the loss of her friend. Tony's engagement to a well-endowed farmer's daughter had completed her chagrin. She wanted no more to do with men.

Morag brought in a tray of tea and biscuits and was introduced. She was gnarled and brown with bright dark eyes, a remnant of the old family re-tainer type, now rapidly becoming obsolete. To Frances' offer of help she shook her grey head.

'Nay, lass, take the neet to settle in. You can start in the morn.'

'She's getting past it,' Margaret explained, when the old woman had gone. 'My health won't permit me to do much and Lesley refuses to have anything to do with the house, so you see how much we need your services.' She looked at Frances anxiously. 'You don't look very robust, and when the twins come up for the summer holidays there'll be a lot to do. They're dear girls, but they're out of doors all the time and no help.'

The twins had not been mentioned when Frances was offered the job and she felt a twinge of resentment. How many more individuals were going to be foisted upon her?

'I'm quite strong and I'm sure I can cope,' she returned, 'but I didn't know there would be so many of you.'

'It's only during the holidays,' Margaret assured her. 'And they do liven the place up.'

'I see. So there's yourself, son and daughter, and Mr Crawford . . .'

'Oh no, you don't have to do anything for Gray,' Mrs Ferguson interrupted. 'He has his own rooms at the top of the tower and a manservant to care for them when he's here. In the winter we all move to our house Glasgow, and if you suit . . . I mean if we get on . . . I hope you'll accompany us.'

'I should like that.'

Already Frances found this moutain retreat a little oppressive. In winter it would be bleak and probably completely cut off by snow.

'I'll do my best to give satisfaction,' she added primly.

Margaret smiled; she had a sweet smile.

'I'm sure you will, I only hope you'll be able to bear with us. We're a rather—how shall I put it?— eccentric family. Ian's a dear, and will do anything to help you feel at home, but Lesley . . .' she paused. 'My daughter is quite unpredictable,' she finished.

That Frances could well believe.

Later Morag was summoned to take her up to her room. This was over the sitting room with the same view of the loch. The furniture was heavy and old-fashioned, the bedstead a tall brass one. Frances

could fancy herself back in Edwardian times except
for the electric stove, which Morag switched on,
saying the nights were still cold. The bathroom was
next door. The old woman was a little dour, and she
eyed Frances critically.

'You're a bit lassie to be on your ain,' she
observed. 'Have you no folks to care for you?'

'My parents are dead.'

'Eh, I'm sorry for that, lass, but dinna greet.' The
dark eyes clouded. 'You'll have a bairn of your own
ere long, I see it in your arms.'

Frances shivered, then laughed. She knew Highland women were reputed to have second sight, but
this was going a bit far, to foretell a baby when she
had not been more than a few hours in the place!

'I haven't come here to get married,' she said
lightly, 'but to work. Now tell me what time you
have meals.'

Morag's eyes were bright again, as she complied.
Left alone, Frances sampled the bathroom, which
contained a huge bath and other fitments, all
equally antiquated, but there was a shower. Returning to her room, she unpacked, and discarding the
light tweed suit she had worn for travelling, put on a
wrapper and went to shower. Rather to her surprise,
the water was hot. Then she dressed in a pale laven-
der dress with a sleeveless cardigan in a deeper
shade. She had abandoned conventional black, not
wishing to emphasise her orphaned state, but her
etceteras, shoes, hose and bag, were sable. She
wore her hair parted in the middle and rolled up in a
knot at her nape. It was dense black, and with her big
eyes and oval face she looked like a young madonna.

Before she left the room, she peered out of the window at the gathering dusk. The reflection of the sky still lightened the water, but the opposite hills were dark humps against the oncoming night. Not exactly a cosy place, she decided, recalling the blossoming orchards of Kent with nostalgia, but she had chosen to come here and she must make the best of it.

Frances lost her way in the maze of passages outside her room. Owing to various alterations from time to time, the connections with the main staircase were winding. She came to what she supposed was the back stairs and went down them, hoping they would lead to the kitchen. At the foot of them, she halted. A carpeted corridor ran left and right with a door at either end, but which went where? While she hesitated the one on her right opened and a man came through, moving with swift impetuous strides. He stopped when he saw Frances, and stared. She stared back. He was the shape and size of the demonic figure on the quayside, but he had changed his wet suit for corded pants and jacket over a navy pullover. His garments were beautifully cut and displayed his lean elegance to full advantage. The face above the polo neck collar was arresting. Bronzed by exposure to weather, the features clear-cut and keen, it was a hawk's face, with an aquiline nose, low brows and jutting chin. The deep-set eyes were grey and piercing, and his hair, neither long nor short with a definite wave, was blond. Frances was put in mind of the Vikings, the sea-rovers, brave, ruthless men, whose restless desire for conquest and loot had taken them all over Europe and as far as the coasts of Canada and Greenland.

She realised she must have strayed into the wrong part of the house.

'I'm afraid I'm trespassing,' she apologised. 'I lost my way.'

His face broke into an unexpectedly sweet smile.

'Never say that,' he said gallantly, his voice was quick and light. 'Such a charming visitor could never be a trespasser.'

His eyes travelled appraisingly over her slender figure, with its high small breasts and narrow waist, noting the fineness of bone structure, her delicate wrists and ankles, and the slender column of her white throat rising from the V of her dress. Frances stiffened; she was not so innocent that she could not read the meaning of that scrutiny, he was assessing her good points. Graham Crawford was susceptible to women and with the glamour of his calling, as she had already surmised, a heartbreaker. She felt a passing pity for Lesley Ferguson in her wet-suit with oil-smeared face. This man would be attracted by sophisticated, smart women and could have his pick of them.

'I'm no visitor,' she said coldly, 'I'm the home help.'

His smile became a grin, disclosing white, even teeth.

'Ah yes, Ian went to fetch you from Mallaig. I bet he was surprised.'

'I don't know, I've no idea what he was expecting.'

'Nothing like you.' His eyes were on her face now, dwelling upon her shadowed eyes, the passionate curve of her lovely mouth.

'You saw me arrive, didn't you?'

'I saw someone arriving, but I didn't stop to look at you. If I had I'd have sent you straight back again.'

Frances' eyes widened in dismay, but she returned with spirit:

'But why, Mr Crawford? I'm nothing to do with you. I'm told you have your own quarters and we needn't even meet. I'm sorry that I've accidentally intruded upon you.'

'I'm not surrounded by barbed wire,' he retorted. 'We all muck in together at times, but you're a most unlikely-looking domestic worker.'

He had known she had been engaged, but like Ian he had expected someone much more ordinary.

'I can't help my looks,' Frances pointed out. 'Does one have to have a special appearance to proclaim one's occupation?'

'Certain types seem to gravitate towards different jobs. "Home help" conjures up a homely, comfortable personality. You're much too decorative.'

'You think I'd do better as a model or an actress? Unfortunately I've no bent towards either, and both professions are overcrowded.'

'The intimacy of the home offers equal scope for your talents, as no doubt you've considered. I gather you have to depend upon them for your livelihood?'

'Yes, but . . .' She paused, wondering what he was implying. He stood beside her, hands in trousers pockets, one shoulder against the wall, and he seemed unable to take his eyes from her face. That direct probing gaze was making her feel uncomfortable.

Suddenly he straightened himself, and his face altered, the eyes narrowing, the mouth becoming stern, all trace of his former gallantry obliterated like flowers before a frost.

'This is an isolated place, Miss what's-your-name, with few distractions. Young Ian is an impressionable youth, and being older than he is I feel it's my duty to protect him from designing females. If you want to stay here, you must keep your distance. I can't have him neglecting his work on your account.'

This wholly unjustifiable attack took her breath away. She understood then what he had meant by using her talents. He thought she was on the lookout for a husband to keep her. An indignant flush rose to her pale cheeks and her eyes sparkled dangerously.

'How dare you!' she said in a tense, low voice. 'You're insulting! You must mix with a very low type of woman, cocottes and adventuresses.' (Wasn't that what they called them in novels?) 'I assure you your precious Ian is perfectly safe from me. You might as well accuse me of having designs upon yourself.'

A gleam of appreciation had come into the hard grey eyes. When Frances was angry she looked beautiful.

'Perhaps you have,' he said softly, 'but I warn you I'm a tough nut to crack.'

'I didn't know you existed until this afternoon.' She clenched her hands, restraining a desire to smack his face—hard. 'I'm not one of your fans.

Belting up the loch like a bat out of hell, nearly overturning us, in a thing that must have cost the earth and serves no useful purpose . . .'

His hand closed over her wrist like a steel band.

'You ignorant woman, Silver Arrow is superb. Say what you like about me, but keep your tongue off her!'

She knew then what was his ruling passion—a machine that would take precedence over any woman in his life. God pity any woman who was fool enough to love him. With an effort she controlled her temper.

'Let me go, Mr Crawford! I'm sorry, I forgot my place.'

'You did.' He dropped her wrist, and she rubbed it against her skirt, feeling sure it was bruised.

'I won't again.' She smiled wanly. 'For the record, my name is Desmond and I came here to work, not to flirt with your employees. But you've no right to make such insinuations. I would ask you to take that back.'

He shook his head, but his eyes were no longer cold, they had a sensual look, and she suddenly wondered if his apprehensions were altogether upon Ian's account.

'No, I'll not take anything back. I was warning you. Any hanky-panky on your part, and out you go.'

'You're not my employer, Mr Crawford.'

'No, I wouldn't be such a fool as to engage you. All the same, I'm the boss here, and what I say goes.'

Frances' colour had receded and she veiled her

eyes meekly with her lashes, but with no idea of how alluring she looked. There was no meekness in her heart. He was, she thought, the most objectionable, arrogant man she had ever encountered—though she had to admit her experience was limited.

'Well, you've certainly clarified my position,' she said demurely, 'but I assure you, you'll have no cause to complain of my conduct.'

An old-fashioned gong boomed through the house, reverberating down the stairs—the summons to supper. Frances turned to go back the way she had come, but she had only gained the first step when she felt his hands on her shoulders.

'Not that way, Miss Desmond, you'll get lost again.' He propelled her towards the opposite door. 'This leads into the hall, the dining room is opposite the drawing room.'

His fingers seemed to burn through the thin stuff of her dress, and Frances became aware that he possessed a powerful sexual magnetism. A tremor ran down her spine that was not all anger. Nor was his hold gentle. He resents me, she thought, as much as Lesley does, but for such a stupid reason. Are there so few girls in this part of the world that he imagines Ian will fall for me?

Freeing one hand, he opened the door and pushed her through it.

'Remember,' he cautioned her.

Holding the door open, she turned to face him.

'For your peace of mind,' her tone was sarcastic, 'I'd have you know I've got a boy-friend back in Kent, and I'm not one to let my fancy rove.'

He need not know that Tony had ditched her.

'Too far away,' was his comment. He looked her up and down and suddenly smiled, that sweet smile which altered his whole face. 'Run along and get your supper, little girl. I expect you're ready for it.'

He closed the door behind her, leaving her choking with sheer rage. He made her feel like an irresponsible teenager.

CHAPTER TWO

FRANCES' life soon settled into a routine. Her duties turned out to be much lighter than she had expected and the big kitchen was fitted with modern labour-saving devices, a large Aga stove which also heated the water and warmed the place, an electric washing machine and dishwasher and a vacuum cleaner. Morag was reluctant to relinquish more of the work than she must, in spite of Frances' willingness to take it over. She acted as kitchenmaid for the older woman, took Mrs Ferguson's breakfast upstairs to her, for she always had it in bed, did her share of the cleaning and prepared the evening meal.

Ian took the motor launch into Mallaig once a week shopping, and sometimes Lesley went with him; once a month he went to Glasgow for stores to replenish the deep-freezer. Morag and Frances were given one whole day off each every week, upon which Morag went to visit relatives in a croft up the glen, but Frances found little to do upon hers. There were tracks over the hills, but she was warned

about going far, because a sudden change in the
weather could envelop them in mist in which she
would lose herself.

She asked one night at supper if it were possible
to bathe in the loch, but Ian told her the water was
much too cold.

'Are you an ardent swimmer?'

Frances shook her head. 'I can't swim at all. I
only splash in the shallows.' She regretted that she
had never learned, for she loved to feel the salt
water on her limbs.

Lesley threw her a look of contempt.

'Then keep clear of the loch, it's deep.'

Frances only saw Gray in the distance during her
first two weeks, but his personality seemed to per-
vade the house. Lesley and Ian talked of him inces-
santly; they seemed obsessed by his doings.

Mrs Ferguson insisted that Frances should go out
for half an hour after lunch every day, saying she
needed exercise and fresh air. She took Caesar with
her upon these rambles along the lakeside. Sometimes the day was clear and sunny, at other times
loch and hills were obscured by wet mist. He was
really Gray's dog, and his master often took him for
long walks in the early morning when he was at
Craig Dhu.

'It's his way of keeping fit,' Ian told her. 'Driving
a speedboat does nothing for the leg muscles.'

She discovered he designed most of the new
models which when completed were brought up to
the loch for trial. Silver Arrow was an improved
design which Gray was taking to America in the late
summer where there were a number of regattas on

the lakes and off shore. He had won many races, but was aiming for world championship. That entailed points for the first six finishers in selected offshore power boat races in different countries. He showed her Silver Arrow when Gray was out of the way. She was a jet-propelled hydroplane with planes attached to her hull, which, Ian explained, enabled her to raise her bow out of the water and skim along its surface. He regaled Frances with a mass of technical jargon to which she listened politely, but could make little of it. He also told her that speedboat racing was a very expensive sport and only the well-to-do could indulge in it. Gray was lucky in having obtained a very wealthy sponsor for his American trip. One day at the end of her first week this man paid them a visit, arriving in what Ian called a 'gin palace' of a motor craft which he had hired during his stay in England. His name was Stuart Lambert, but they all called him 'Stu'. Lesley and Ian went down to the harbour to launch Silver Arrow, which Gray was demonstrating. Mrs Ferguson with Frances in attendance watched from the window. Not that there was much to see except a great plume of spray as the boat went past. Later Frances glimpsed the party standing on the jetty which included a very soignée young lady in the smartest of yachting outfits. Gray did not introduce them to his visitors. He took them up to his eyrie at the top of the tower, and his man Murdoch toiled after them carrying cases of drinks. Later Ian told Frances the young lady was Samantha Lambert, old Stu's daughter.

'She's got her eye on Gray,' he said despondently. 'And I suppose it would be a good match for him, she's rolling, but if he gets married things will never be the same again.'

Frances did not know what she would have done without Ian. He was her mainstay and informant, always ready to help and explain. Inevitably she saw a lot of him, at mealtime and in the evenings which they both spent with his mother. Gray had an office adjoining the boat sheds, and Lesley, besides being a mechanic, could type. She handled Gray's correspondence. She always spent her evenings there, in the hope of seeing him, but Gray flashed in and out of Craig Dhu like a meteor, usually leaving a trail of havoc behind him. This and that had not been done or had been done wrongly, some emergency had arisen that must have immediate attention, then he was gone again—Glasgow, Edinburgh, London—only to return without warning with a fresh batch of complaints.

'Is it possible to please him?' Frances asked Ian after a flaming row about some missing spares which she had inadvertently overheard.

'Oh yes, he's very fair, and he gives praise where it's due, but it was my fault about the spares, I forgot to order them.'

She herself had not spoken to him since that first evening.

On her second day off, Ian asked her if she would like to go with him to Mallaig for the weekly shop, and she accepted eagerly. She awoke to a beautiful early summer morning, and rose with a pleasurable sense of anticipation, because it would be a change to see some shops and people. Craig Dhu, being off the beaten track, was rarely penetrated by tourists.

Margaret Ferguson had given her some small commissions the night before as they were to make an early start. She wore a grey pleated skirt with a white knitted top, white sandals, and carried a white cardigan in case it was cold on the water. She did her hair in its usual knot, surmounted by a white woolly cap to keep it tidy. She was bare-legged, for getting in and out of boats played havoc with hose, and she hoped she might have time to paddle on the beach, because she loved to walk on wet sand with the wavelets curling round her ankles.

She came down to breakfast to find only Morag present, the others having gone out earlier.

'Oh dear, am I late?' she asked anxiously.

'He's wanting to be off,' the old woman said dourly. 'I've cooked your victuals.' She dumped a plate of egg and bacon down in front of Frances. 'You be needing more than toast if you're going on the water, and I ken you won't touch porridge.'

Frances had steadfastly refused the oatmeal which Morag considered was the only fit breakfast dish.

Frances thanked her and attacked the meal. Ian had not said anything about starting so soon the night before. Unlike Gray he would not mind waiting while she ate something, she thought; they had all day before them, so there could not be any desperate haste.

When she had finished she rose to put the crockery in the dishwasher, but Morag said:

'Best be off, lass, that one don't like to be kept waiting.' She was looking at Frances oddly.

'Another five minutes won't matter,' Frances declared, but she left the crocks and ran out into fresh morning sunshine.

The middle-aged motor launch Ian usually used was nowhere to be seen, instead a newer, smaller craft was moored to the jetty. As she stood wondering, Gray Crawford came striding towards her from the office.

'You've taken your time,' he grumbled. 'Hop in.'

She stared at him in some confusion and made no move.

'Well, don't you want to go to Mallaig?' he snapped.

'Yes, but . . . where's Ian?'

'Where I sent him.' He threw her an inimical glance. 'Don't stand havering, woman!'

Without a by-your-leave, he picked her up and dumped her over the side into the boat, then he sprang in beside her and cast off. The engine started with its familiar chug-chug, and the fast little craft shot out into the loch. There were two seats for'ard like the front ones in a car and they were side by side. Frances was dismayed by this change of plan. She could not imagine Gray doing the weekly shop, and he could not be going merely to accommodate her. She sighed despondently, for she had been looking forward to a long, leisurely day. Ian had suggested they lunch out, but this man would not want to linger. She looked at him sideways. In spite of the windscreen the speed of their going blew back the fair hair from his forehead, giving him more than ever a Viking look. He wore cord pants, a white shirt and a blue blazer, which lent a nautical touch to his appearance. He gave the impression of a greyhound straining at the leash, as streamlined and as elegant.

As the loch opened out into the sound, he slackened speed and turned to look at her. The fresh morning air had whipped colour into her cheeks and brightened her eyes, her white outfit contrasted with the glossy darkness of her hair. Feeling selfconscious under his scrutiny, she said to break the silence:

'This is an alteration in arrangements, isn't it?'

'Yes,' he spoke curtly. 'Were you looking forward to Ian's company?'

'Well, he does know what's wanted and I have some extra shopping to do, but I expect you'll have some business to attend to while I do it?'

Because why else had he come?

'No. Like yourself I'm having a day off.'

The sea was calm as a pond, a deep blue reflecting a cloudless sky, a perfect day for the seashore.

'Then perhaps you'll be visiting some friends?'

'Friends in Mallaig?' He sounded scornful. 'Do you object to my society?'

'Of course not.' She saw her unhurried browse round vanishing. 'But it'll be tedious for you.'

'Does Ian find it so?'

'I don't know, I haven't been with him before.'

'Really?' He sounded disbelieving.

'I've been here a fortnight and this is the first time I've left Craig Dhu.'

'So long? I must be slipping.'

She looked at him doubtfully. 'I don't know what you mean, Mr Crawford.'

'Gray, please.'

'Oh no!' She could not be so familiar with him.

'Why not?'

'Well . . . you're the boss.'

The grey eyes crinkled. 'Does that make me un-approachable?'

'Yes, but . . .'

'No buts. You'll call me Gray, that's an order. Everyone else does except when they use less polite epithets. We're a democratic institution at Craig Dhu.'

'Oh, I thought it was a dictatorship.'

'Did you now? Don't be impertinent, Frances.' She was surprised he knew her first name, for during the past two weeks he seemed to have forgotten her existence. 'I think it's time we got to know each other.'

'Is that necessary, Mr . . .' she caught his eye, 'Gray? I mean, our paths don't cross.'

'They have this morning, and I'm responsible for the staff at Craig Dhu. I'm told you're proving very satisfactory.'

'Thank you, I'm glad to know that.' She was pleased.

'Except in one particular,' he added ominously.

'I'm sorry, where have I failed?'

He looked away from her, intent upon his steering.

'Ian. You see too much of him.'

'But he's always there,' she pointed out, thinking he was absurdly protective of his assistant. 'I must talk to someone—do you expect me to sit alone in my room in the evenings?'

'It might be as well. You're distracting him.'

'I'm sure I'm not.'

He looked at her accusingly. 'He forgot to order those spares, which is most unlike him. He's showing every symptom of a boy in love.'

'That's ridiculous,' Frances cried indignantly. 'I'm sure you're wrong, Mr ... Gray. I've only known him two weeks.'

He threw her an oblique glance. 'It can happen in a day. Have you told him about the boy in Kent?'

Perturbed by his remarks, she looked blank, forgetting what she had told him. Recovering quickly, she said hastily:

'No, my private life is my own concern.'

'That depends ... heard from him recently?'

Frances had only had two letters since she had been in Scotland, both business communications, and she wondered if Gray scrutinised the mail when it arrived, but Lesley attended to his letters, so it was unlikely.

'The posts are very slow up here,' she said carefully. 'I've heard ... once.'

'You must find that very trying.'

'I'm striving to bear up.'

'We must try to keep you contented. Perhaps he would like to pay you a visit.'

'Would that be possible?' she asked uncertainly; her fiction about Tony might be difficult to maintain.

'Quite, there's plenty of room in the house.'

'It's very kind of you to suggest it,' she said brightly. 'But he has a job, so I'm afraid he couldn't get away until he has his holidays late in the summer.' When Gray would have gone to America.

'But surely he could manage a weekend,' Gray persisted.

His keen grey eyes had a mischievous sparkle and she feared he saw through her fabrications. She should have told the truth, that Tony had let her down so she was immune from masculine advances, but it was too late now, and she decided to launch a counter-offensive.

'It's a long way for a weekend. Are you wanting him here to . . . er . . . distract me from Ian? I'm not at all interested in Ian.'

'Poor Ian, but his presence might effect a cure.'

'I don't think lovesickness is ever cured that way,' she said, thinking of Lesley and her hopeless passion for the man beside her. 'But I'm sure you're exaggerating.'

'You're much too good-looking,' Gray said slowly. 'If I were your fiancé, I'd never let you out of my sight.'

'Please don't flatter me,' she requested quickly, aware of a sudden quickening of her pulse. 'I'm afraid you have a jealous disposition, Gray.'

'I resent others' claims to my possessions,' he said shortly, 'and I know how to take care of them. But have you no family?'

Glad to change the subject, Frances told him of her orphaned state, her need to earn her living in any post she could obtain.

'I only have one living relative,' she concluded, 'a grandfather who refuses to acknowledge me. He disapproved of my mother's marriage and dropped her. But none of this can be very interesting to you.'

'I like to know my employees' background,' he

returned coolly. 'You know the Fergusons, I suppose?'

'Aren't they relations?'

'They're not, but Crawfords are responsible for them. Margaret's husband was killed testing one of our boats, so the firm felt we had a moral obligation to take care of the widow and her children, though James had only himself to blame. The accident occurred as a direct contravention of orders.'

That started a new train of thought. 'Is speedboat racing very dangerous?' she asked.

He shrugged his shoulders. 'Men have been killed, but so they have at other sports, to use a cliché, no more risky than crossing the road—but we'll never get there if we continue to dawdle like this.'

He turned his attention to his driving and the boat gathered speed.

Mallaig is not a pretty place, but it has character; conspicuous is a long row of whitewashed fishermen's cottages facing the harbour with a bleak hill behind them. Fish is its main occupation, and now the tourist trade. Sheep wander in its streets and it has an enormous population of seagulls, which follow the ferries all the way to Skye. That island and the nearer Eigg and Rhum are features of the landscape.

When they had landed, Gray handed Frances Ian's grocery list and told her to leave it at the shop he named to be made up and they would take it down to the boat, and then do her own shopping.

'I've booked lunch at the West Highland Hotel,' he told her. 'I'll meet you there at twelve-thirty.

Okay?'

'Oh, but I didn't expect . . .' Frances began, considerably taken aback.

'A treat for your day out,' he explained, 'to compensate for depriving you of Ian's company. You'd better get on with your shopping or you'll be late.'

He strode away and Frances proceeded to sample what shops there were and execute Mrs Ferguson's commissions. She was perturbed by Gray's insistence that there was something between Ian and herself. She liked the lad, but that was all he was to her, though he was about her own age, and she did not believe he had any sentimental feelings towards her; he was much too absorbed in his boats. But there was danger in propinquity and they were thrown very much together. Perhaps she had better introduce him to the Tony myth to warn him off, but she hated dissembling, and she was already in difficulties over that—moreover, it seemed vain to suppose the young man had fallen for her. She would never have thought of it if Gray had not kept harping upon that theme.

She had learned that the family at Craig Dhu were deeply indebted to Gray and his firm financially and for their employment. Being of a despotic turn of mind he probably felt he owned them, but he did not own her. Possibly that was what was needling him; he did not like a foreign element threatening his sovereignty, he wanted to come first with all of them. But Ian being a normal young man would sooner or later find a girl he wanted to marry, unlike Lesley, who worshipped Gray, to the exclusion of anyone else, though not necessarily herself. His motive in accompanying her today might be a wish to subjugate her also. He could not bear to be other than the sun around which his satellites revolved, but if that were so, he had another think coming! She was no susceptible teenager to succumb to a handsome hydrofoil racer. She had been in love and had her love rejected, and she was not going to become involved again with either Gray or Ian.

Yet when she turned her footsteps towards the West Highland, conspicuous in its commanding position above the harbour, she was conscious of pleasurable excitement. Gray's society was stimulating and a meal out would be a change. She wished she was dressed more smartly and had put on hose, but with so many casually clad young people about it did not greatly matter.

As she came up the steps to the entrance, between steep grassy banks upon which she was amused to see a ewe and two lambs were grazing—a cheap way to mow them—she discerned her host seated outside the hotel on a narrow verandah which flanked the front of it, on which were set out tables and chairs. He stood up as she approached with an ironic glance at her shopping basket filled with Margaret Ferguson's small parcels.

'Been busy?'

'Yes, I think I've got everything.'

Unaccountably she was breathless, and her heart had jumped at the sight of him; he looked so lithe and debonair against the background of the dining room windows, his grey eyes slightly mocking, though his smile was welcoming. Undoubtedly Gray

Crawford had something which could stir a woman's heart.

A waiter appeared and he beckoned to him.

'What will you drink?'

'Medium sherry, please.'

Frances sat down. A view over the sea was spread before them, the tips of the mountains on Skye just visible on the horizon.

'The road to the Isles,' she murmured.

'Yes, and this is the end of it—and then over the sea to Skye.'

The waiter brought her drink, and a beer for Gray, and he talked about the '45, the raising of Prince Charlie's flag at Loch Shiel, and his departure from Scotland a year later never to return.

'Would you have been a Jacobite?' Frances asked.

Gray laughed and shook his head. 'Lost causes don't appeal to me, I'm no romantic. One has only one life and it's up to one to get the most out of it.'

This hedonist view rather shocked her, but confirmed her opinion that Graham Crawford was an egoist intent only upon making his mark upon the world through the success of Silver Arrow.

They went inside for lunch and though it was summer a log fire burned in the entrance hall, and its warmth was not unwelcome. In the powder room, Frances repaired her make-up, and wondered how many girls Gray had brought here for entertainment. She was sure he was by no means an ascetic.

They had a table in the window with the same fine view. Gray was a charming host, treating her as though she was a special guest and not his employees' home help. He was no snob, nor did he enlarge upon his exploits or his boats, though she asked several leading questions, which he evaded skilfully. So he was no boaster either. She did learn that his parents were still alive, though his father was about to retire from the business, and he had a married sister whose husband was managing director, being responsible for it during Gray's frequent absences.

'I can't bear being cooped up indoors,' he confessed, 'but Sandy doesn't like speedboats, except to sell them, so we work well together, except when he grumbles at me for overspending.'

Frances recalled that Ian had told her speedboat racing was a rich man's sport and wondered if Gray were too extravagant for his firm's resources, but that was no concern of hers, as he would be the first to tell her.

She was conscious that he looked at her a great deal and hoped that he liked what he saw, but it might be he was trying to discover what Ian saw in her, since he persisted in thinking the boy fancied her.

'What do you want to do now?' he asked, when they reached the coffee stage.

'I suppose I ought to go back.' She looked wistfully at the sea. If she had been alone she would have wandered round the little town, but she could not expect him to wait about for her.

'But it's your day off and it's not nearly over yet. We might go and look at the white sands of Morar. I keep a car here, it's useful for getting about.'

'I'd love that,' she said eagerly.

Gray's car was what she expected, a low-slung powerful sports model. He drove her up the hill out of Mallaig, and over the river between Loch Morar and the sea, that cascades in falls on either side of the road. The rhododendrons, which are prolific in that country, were beginning to come into bloom, and there were little fresh water pools full of yellow waterlilies. He took the road towards Arisaig with the estuary to their right, and the sands actually were white. They left the car and walked down to the water's edge.

'It's lovely,' she exclaimed. 'I wish . . .' she stopped.

She could not express a desire to paddle in his august company, but he seemed to divine her thought.

'Take off your sandals, if you want to walk on the sand, then you won't get them wet, but don't go too far.'

She slipped her feet out of them, and he picked them up. 'I'm going back to the car, I've some papers I want to look at.'

He went off carrying her sandals, and Frances ran barefooted through the clear shallow water and over the white sand. The clear, pure air went to her head like wine, the wide expanse of sea and sky gave a delicious sense of complete freedom. She took off her cap and her hair fell about her shoulders, stirred by the breeze. Intriguing shells caught her attention, and she began to collect them, filling her discarded cap, forgetting completely whom she was with, 'Speed, bonny boat, like a bird on the wing,' she sang softly. 'Over the sea to Skye', and waved her hand to the islands, of which there was a glorious view.

Gray's voice recalled her from her enchanted world, with the realisation that she was not behaving like a home help.

'Come back—the tide comes in like a racehorse and it's on the turn!'

He had left the car and had followed her some distance along the water's edge. She came back towards him wondering for how long he had been watching her, still clutching her cap full of trophies, her exhilaration fading.

'Whatever must you think of me?' she cried as she came within earshot.

'That there's been a mistake in your birth certificate. You must be thirteen, not—what is it?— twenty-three.'

He was smiling with obvious amusement as he surveyed her, and she became painfully conscious of her splashed skirt and flowing hair.

'I'm sorry, Gray,' she said humbly. 'This is an enchanted place and something, I don't know what, got into me. I . . . I must look a mess.'

'You look like a sea nymph, only you've too many clothes on.' He reached out and took hold of a tress of her hair, drawing her towards him. 'Not many girls have hair like this nowadays.' His eyes glinted. 'So the aloof Miss Desmond is human after all? I wonder just how human.'

Something in his expression caused her to blush. She jerked her hair out of his hold, and asked for her sandals which she saw he was carrying. He dropped them at her feet, and as she stooped for them, said blandly, 'Let me assist you.'

He bent down and held one ready for her to put her foot in it, and as she did so, his fingers lingered on her instep as he fastened it. He had sunk down upon one knee, oblivious of the wet sand, and his touch lingered still longer on the second one. Frances had narrow feet with a high instep of which she was rather vain, and as Gray's fingers caressed them, for that was what he was doing, tremors shot up her legs to her spine. She wanted to pull away, but feared to lose her balance; as it was, she had to clutch at his shoulder for support. He had discarded his jacket, and the feel of his firm muscles through his thin shirt caused her another thrill. She feared he knew how he was affecting her, and felt a stab of anger, but she could not expect him to show her respect after her hoyden exhibition of herself.

'Thank you,' she said with heightened colour when both sandals were in place. 'I must apologise . . .'

'Whatever for?' He stood up, dusting the sand from his knee. 'It was a pleasure to watch you being young and natural instead of in the rather severe pose you normally assume.' He reached for her cap. 'We'll find a bag for these trophies of yours, so you can put your cap on again. Charming though you look, the good people of Mallaig might misinterpret what we've been doing if they see you in disarray.'

'I must have been crazy.' Frances tried to twist up her hair.

'You'll find that easier to do in the car out of the wind.' The breeze had blown a strand of it across his face, and he removed it almost reverently. 'Why don't you wear it loose?'

'Not very suitable for a home help.'

'But you're not on duty now, neither am I. So we can indulge ourselves.'

She shot him a wary glance; there was a wicked gleam in the grey eyes.

'You started it by telling me to take my sandals off.'

'Ah, I shall know what to do when I want you to unbend.'

'I shan't forget myself again,' she said frigidly as they reached the car.

'Oh, what a pity!' Gray laughed, then he became serious. 'Don't worry, Fran, I haven't time to pursue you, amusing though that might be. I took time off today because I was becoming edgy, and I did have an errand to do in Mallaig.'

His abbreviation of her name suggested an intimacy which she did not want, and she said icily as she climbed into the car:

'I've no intention of providing you with amusement.'

He laughed again. 'Pax, Fran, don't spoil a pleasant day by mounting your high horse, we mayn't ever have another.'

She found his last statement depressing, but assured herself that the less she saw of him the better; he was a disturbing person.

'Yes, it has been pleasant,' she agreed formally, 'and I must thank you very, very much.'

He stood beside the open door wearing an inscrutable expression and she had a moment's panic that he was going to demand a more tangible form of gratitude. Her eyes were on his firm, well-shaped mouth, and a quiver of excitement ran through her at the thought of its pressure on her lips. Instantly she suppressed the wanton urge, and the tense moment passed. Gray rummaged in the trunk and presented her with a polythene bag for her shells, and she plaited her hair, fixing it firmly under her cap.

'There,' she said, 'Miss Desmond is herself again.'

'Quite so,' he drawled as he took his place beside her. 'And Mr Crawford has remembered his objective.'

She glanced at him curiously as the car shot back on to the road. His profile was set and stern. Had he also felt the urge that had risen in her when he stood by the car door, as if there were some physical affinity between them? If he had he had firmly repressed it, but she decided it was unlikely. He probably kissed girls casually and carelessly when the opportunity presented itself, and only her lack of response had checked him. His only real love was Silver Arrow, and that was what he meant by his objective.

The voyage back was without incident, and Gray was taciturn. He seemed to have withdrawn from her entirely. Frances watched the sky flame over the sea as the sun began to sink, aware of a pleasant melancholy.

'I always feel a little sad when the sun goes down,' she said.

'The death of each day's life,' he quoted, and she was surprised, for she had not thought Gray would read the classics, 'but that referred to sleep that knits up the ravelled sleave of care, and after all that fresh air you should be ready for your bed, or do you lie awake yearning for the boy in Kent?'

'Of course not,' she said crossly, needled by his tone. 'I'm a practical girl.'

Whereat he laughed and she wondered why he was amused.

Lesley was waiting for them on the jetty wearing a light sweater and jeans.

'You're very late,' she greeted them, as she caught the painter. 'We began to fear you'd had an accident.'

'In this old tub?' Gray asked scornfully, leaping out of the boat, and holding out his hand to assist Frances. 'I've been showing Fran some of the beauties of Scotland.'

'How nice for her!' Lesley's deep voice grated. 'Ian will come down to collect the stores, and I hope you've remembered Mrs Ferguson's commissions, Miss Desmond.'

'Yes, I think I've got everything,' Frances told her, feeling guilty. A day off did not include the evening, and she was too late to help with supper. Gray reached out and took her shopping bag from her.

'I'll bring this up to the house for you.'

'Surely Miss Desmond is capable of carrying it herself,' Lesley said sharply.

'I don't doubt it, but I prefer to carry it for her.'

Frances was on the edge of the quay as they moved away, with Lesley between her and Gray. She was never able to recall exactly what happened. It seemed Lesley tripped and stumbled against her.

She knew she was falling, clutched at nothingness, and then the waters of the loch closed over her head.

CHAPTER THREE

'SHE'S breathing regularly now.'

Frances heard the words as she drifted back to consciousness. She found she was lying on her back on the floor in front of an electric stove in Gray's office, wrapped in a travelling rug. There were pools of water all around her which Lesley was swabbing up. Someone—Gray, she saw with surprise—was kneeling beside her. When she opened her eyes, he turned her on to her side, facing the fire, and in answer to a query from Lesley said solemnly:

'The textbooks say the subject should assume a coma position after administering artificial respiration. She's not warm enough, get that coat of mine that's hanging up on the door.' He turned back the rug and began to rub her feet.

A sheepskin coat was thrown over her, and Frances caught a glimpse of Lesley's face as she bent above her. It was white and strained, and she wondered vaguely why she was looking so upset. She went away and returned with a glass which she held to Frances' lips, raising her head with her other hand. It was whisky mixed with hot water, and Frances spluttered as she swallowed some of it. It ran like fire through her veins, warming, reviving. Gray covered her feet and stood up.

'Nip up to the house,' he ordered tersely. 'Bring her some dry clothes. Find Murdoch and tell him to bring me some too. Tell Morag to warm Frances' bed—hurry!'

Lesley hesitated. 'You go, you need a hot bath. I can look after Frances.'

'I think not.'

There was such emphasis on the three words that Lesley wilted. Then she was gone.

Gray crouched beside her, drawing the wet mass of her hair away from her neck and shoulders and spreading it fanwise over the rug. He picked up the glass which Lesley had put down, and raising her so that she was supported against his shoulder, held it to her mouth.

'Drink some more.'

Obediently she took a sip. 'Ugh, it's nasty!'

'Nasty? It's the best Glenlivet!'

He had torn off his soaking shirt and his bronzed torso was bare except for a faint golden down on his chest. One naked arm held her closely against him, while he offered the glass. Disturbed by the close contact, she said faintly:

'I fell in the loch, didn't I?'

'You did.' His face was grim.

'You jumped in after me?'

His arm tightened about her. 'Did you think I could let you drown?'

'I . . . I was careless . . .'

Gray said nothing to that, but his face became even grimmer. Frances made a movement of withdrawal.

'I . . . I'm better now. I'd like to sit up.'

There was an ancient armchair near the fire, in which Gray very occasionally relaxed, when he was working there. He lifted her to put her into it, and as he did so, the rug slipped from her shoulder; beneath it she was naked, and she wondered anxiously who had stripped her. Her soaked clothing was in a pile on the floor. Her uncovered white flesh made contact with Gray's and he suddenly bent his head and pressed his lips to it. An electric shock shot through her, leaving every nerve tingling. Never had she imagined a man's proximity could so violently affect her.

'Please, Gray,' she murmured, and there was appeal in voice and eyes. She was begging him not to exploit the powerful force that was igniting between them.

'Woman, you're a menace,' he said hoarsely.

She could have retorted that he was even more so to her, but she was too spent for banter. She was seeing again the dim quay, Lesley's taut figure beside her as she slipped, the hand extended but not to succour her . . . no, surely Lesley could not have deliberately pushed her in? Mad jealous she might have been because Gray had spent the day with her, but she wouldn't go that far . . . or would she? She shivered, and Gray sat down in the chair with her upon his knees, crushing her close to him so that the heat from his body could penetrate hers.

'What the devil's keeping that girl?' he muttered.

Frances could feel the strong beat of his heart next to hers.

Then they heard voices and running feet and the room was full of people. Frances was wrapped in more blankets, while Murdoch assisted Gray into dry clothes. Feebly she protested:

'I can't walk in all these swathings!'

'You're not going to walk,' Gray told her, and it was he who carried her up to the house, while Murdoch and Lesley brought their wet garments. The last glimmering of twilight lay over the loch, turning the water to pewter; the first stars gleamed above the mountains. Light streaming from the house lit their path. Frances murmured against Gray's shoulder:

'It's a beautiful world, I'm glad I'm still in it.'

'If you're staying here, you must learn to swim,' was his prosaic rejoinder.

He had not known she could not swim, but Lesley did, and again she shivered, feeling she was wading into tides of emotion which were too strong for her. Could one hate a rival enough to want to see her dead? But she was not Lesley's rival in any real sense. She had merely caught Gray's passing fancy, and if she judged him correctly it would be only a fleeting one.

Frances suffered no ill effects from her ducking, though Morag fussed over her and insisted that she have her breakfast in bed next morning. She got up in the afternoon and found to her dismay that Gray was coming to supper. When he honoured them with his presence, the meal was formalised into dinner; everyone changed, and efforts were made to provide him with a succulent meal. Frances did her share of the preparations feeling slightly contemptuous. Was it really necessary to make such a god of him, pandering to his already inflated ego? True, they were all dependent upon his goodwill, but did he appreciate sycophancy? She owed him her life and she would have to find an opportunity to thank him properly. She hoped he would not try to make capital out of that, for any advances from him would worsen the situation between herself and Lesley, and she did not want to encourage him, but she could not ignore the debt she owed him.

She changed into a plain black dress for dinner with a modest V-neckline and short sleeves. With her white skin and dense black hair she was a symphony in ebony and ivory. By contrast, Lesley appeared in a full-skirted flame-coloured creation, but in spite of her flamboyant dress she seemed subdued and kept throwing nervous glances towards Gray. Ian, who was perceptive, marked her demeanour.

'Has Lesley done something wrong, Gray? She seems scared of you.'

'Lesley knows what she did, but I don't tell tales,' was the blunt rejoinder. 'Since it appears that our lady help cannot swim that must be rectified immediately. I'll have no one living at Craig Dhu who can't.'

Frances glanced at his stern face uncertainly. Did he mean she was going to be dismissed?

'I'm sorry, I didn't realise that was a necessary qualification when I took the job,' she said awkwardly.

'It didn't occur to me to ask,' Margaret admitted, 'but of course, with having to travel by boat and the loch being so deep, I suppose it is important.' She looked at Frances kindly. 'A shame if you have to leave when you were settling in so well, and I'm sure we'll never get anyone else to replace you.'

Frances was dismayed. She was settling in, as Mrs Ferguson said, and she was finding the life and the company there fascinating. She looked reproachfully at Gray's implacable face. Yesterday he had seemed so friendly and now he was using this paltry excuse to be rid of her, but perhaps it was not really so paltry; but for him she would have drowned, and it could not have been much fun for him having to pull her out. He had called her a menace, but what he really meant was that she might become a distraction, diverting his concentration on his boat. The remedy for that was simple; he only had to avoid her as she would avoid him in future. Or was he thinking of Ian? That young man had been terribly distressed by the accident and his solicitude gave point to Gray's suspicions. It was all so absurd that her job was threatened by emotions which she had had no wish to arouse.

Ian said: 'Couldn't Fran learn to swim?'

'Where can she learn?' his mother asked. 'The loch isn't suitable, and I don't know where there's a swimming pool, and who could teach her?'

'It shouldn't take long,' Lesley observed. 'She's got the right build for a swimmer. There's that little lochan in a hollow in the hill that the twins use. They bullied Murdoch into clearing it of weed. It's quite shallow and wouldn't be too cold.'

Her eyes met Frances' with apology in them, and Frances realised she was trying to make amends. Lesley Ferguson had reckless impulses and a passionate nature, but she was not wicked. She was ashamed of what her jealousy had led her into trying to do.

'Yes, I remember the place,' Gray nodded. 'It might serve.'

'And I can teach her,' Ian said eagerly.

'You will not.' The grey eyes flashed. 'Neither will Lesley.' He smiled at Frances. 'I claim that privilege myself.'

They all looked astonished.

'But . . . but will you have time?' Lesley protested, not liking the proposal at all.

Frances, disconcerted, added quickly: 'I wouldn't dream of putting you to so much trouble.'

'You'd rather leave us?'

So it was an ultimatum. Looking down at her plate, she said quietly: 'I'd hate to have to do that.'

'I'm not going to risk having you near drowned again,' Gray told her firmly. 'I can spare half an hour each day after lunch. I believe you take a walk at that time and if there's any sun the water will be warmer in the afternoon.'

Frances was surprised that he knew her daily routine; she had yet to learn that there was little that went on at Craig Dhu that he did not know.

'I expect Les can lend you a swimsuit,' he went on, glancing meaningly at the other girl.

'I haven't any fancy bikinis,' Lesley told him with a touch of malice, 'only plain regulation black.'

'I'm sure that would do beautifully,' Frances accepted gratefully. She did not want to display herself in the couple of bands most girls wore for swimming. Again she wondered who had stripped her of her clothes, and as if she read her thought, Lesley said:

'You hadn't much on when Gray revived you with the kiss of life.'

Mrs Ferguson looked astonished and Frances blushed.

'The what, dear?'

'Artificial respiration mouth-to-mouth,' Lesley told her.

'Oh, really? I thought it was done by pressing the ribs.'

'It's a more modern method and more effective,' Gray informed her. He was watching Frances with a wicked gleam in his eyes—it amused him to embarrass her, she suspected. She glanced at his strong, handsome mouth, and looked hastily away.

'You seemed to have had fun bringing me round,' she said coldly.

'It wasn't funny at all, we were too anxious.'

She noticed he said 'we'; so Lesley had repented of her violent action when faced with its consequence.

'I'm sure I'm very, very grateful to you *both*,' she said earnestly. 'I owe you my life.'

'Thank you,' Lesley murmured. 'You're generous, Fran.'

It was the first time she had called her other than Miss Desmond.

'All in the day's work,' Gray declared cheerfully. 'She isn't the first I've pulled out of the loch, and I don't suppose she'll be the last, but if she falls in again she won't sink, when I've done my stuff. I'll get Murdoch to look at that pool in the morning, put a bit of duckboard along the edge where it'll be muddy—and I'll expect you there, Fran, at two-thirty sharp, even if it's raining.'

It did not rain, it was a mild and sunny afternoon. Frances found the pool, which was in a fold of the hillside, sparkling in the sunshine. The deeper end of it was completely clear and to the side of it was a small log cabin roofed with turf where bathers could leave their clothes. It was surrounded on three sides by rhododendron bushes, which grew well in that country, and the huge magenta heads were coming into bloom. At the further end of the pool, where the water oozed into marsh, was a spread of yellow waterlilies. It was a favourite resort of the twins, whom she had yet to meet, and they must have spent some time and effort in embellishing it, for there was even a plank pier running out into the water.

Frances arrived first, wearing the swimsuit Lesley had provided under her dress and carrying a towel. Her hair was confined in a rubber cap. She stood by the water feeling a little foolish, for it did not seem as if Gray were going to turn up. Then she saw him coming striding down the hillside with Caesar bounding beside him, and her heart gave a lurch. Bareheaded, in casual shirt and slacks, his throat exposed, the sun gilding his hair, he again reminded her of some Nordic god or mythological hero— Baldur the Beautiful, or Siegfried of the sagas.

He came to stand beside her and looked with amusement at the pool.

'Those young hussies made themselves very free with my property,' he remarked. 'You haven't met them yet. They're nice kids, but a bit presumptuous. They must have got round old Murdoch to do all

that work for them, unbeknown to me. Well, it's
going to be useful to us now.'

He produced a couple of armbands which he inflated.

'These will help you to keep up,' he explained.
'I'll just drop my clothes in the hut and then we'll
get going.'

It took Frances a week to acquire a modest
breaststroke. They were lucky to have a period of
real summer weather, all too rare in Scotland. All
her life Frances was to look back on those golden
afternoons with nostalgia—the blue water and bluer
sky, the flamboyant blooms of the rhododendrons,
the frieze of waterlilies, and Gray Crawford, bare
and bronzed except for his trunks, his strong hands
ever ready to support her when she threatened to
sink, his low encouraging voice, his endless patience,
which was surprising, for he was not a patient man.
She had feared he would quickly become irritated
with her feeble efforts, though actually they were
not feeble at all. She had long arms and a good
breadth of shoulder, and he instilled such confidence
into her that she made fast progress. It seemed as if
he were willing her to swim, so swim she did. At the
end of the week he told her:

'I have to go to Glasgow tomorrow, but you can
manage on your own now. Don't let it drop. Bring
Caesar with you when you come to practise. He'll
guard you and pull you out if you get into difficulties, but you won't. Swimming is something
which once acquired you never forget.'

They had come out of the water, and pulling off
her cap, Frances let her hair fall about her shoul-

ders. It fell nearly to her waist, covering her like a cloak. She had wrapped her towel about her middle.

'I seem to be forever in your debt,' she said gratefull. 'You're very good to me, Gray, and I don't know why.'

Why indeed should he concern himself with his dependents' home help?

'It's nothing,' he said lightly. 'People who live near water should be able to swim, but if you really feel indebted to me,' he came closer with his eyes on her mouth, 'there's a graceful way of saying thank you.'

Her heart began to race suffocatingly fast.

'You mean . . . you'd like me to kiss you?'

He laughed, amused by her naïveté.

'I don't usually ask, I take, but I'd like you to give.'

It cost her an effort to raise her arms and put them around his neck. A kiss meant nothing, but she was strangely reluctant, perhaps because to her it would mean something. She had never been free with her kisses, even with Tony she had been reserved. But Tony had never been demanding; he had thought passion was something that should be restrained until after the wedding. Gray, she felt instinctively, had no inhibitions, and she might be starting what she could not control. The towel slipped from about her—she always seemed to be in a state of undress when she contacted Gray—and as his arms closed round her there was only the thin top of her swimsuit between their bodies. He held her tightly against him, and her hair enveloped them, as their lips met in a long, close pressure. Her

whole body seemed to melt into his, and she could
feel the hard muscles of his thighs against her softer
flesh. Then, almost violently, he pushed her away
from him.

'Thank you . . . Fran . . .' he said shakily. 'That
was . . . very sweet, but . . . Oh, go and put your
clothes on, girl, or I won't answer for myself!'

Feeling vaguely rebuffed, she ran from him into
the shelter of the log hut. She was shaking, and her
whole body seemed aflame. Gray Crawford was
dynamite!

When she had managed to compose herself,
donned her clothes, and come out again, she found
that he had gone.

Dutifully Frances came again the next afternoon,
but the sun went in and the mere seemed unbearably melancholy under a grey sky without his
presence. Caesar too seemed to miss him, for he
prowled along the water's edge whimpering. The
plaintive cry of a curlew added to her feeling of de-
solation. She stayed in the water for only a short
while, as it was cold, and they returned together a
disconsolate pair. She would not come again unless
she could persuade Ian or Lesley to accompany her.
The place was too empty when she was on her own.

Gray was gone two days and returned in the Lamberts' super launch. This time he invited the Fergusons and Frances to join the party for drinks.
Margaret excused herself, saying she did not like the
stairs up to Gray's eyrie, and she felt out of place
among the jet set.

'But you go, Fran,' she bade her, when Frances

suggested she should stay with her. 'You're young, you can take it, and it'll be an education for you to meet Gray's pals.'

Was there a subtle meaning behind her words? Frances had noticed Gray seemed to be partial to her help, and she wanted her to realise she had no part in his world.

Frances wanted to go, not to meet the Lamberts, but to see Gray's quarters which were out of bounds to any but Murdoch, except by invitation. They were in the top half of the old tower, the most ancient part of the building, approach by the original stone spiral stairs. The accommodation comprised two floors, the lower portion being divided into his bedroom, Murdoch's cubbyhole, a kitchen and a bathroom. The upper one was one big sitting room, the enlarged windows looking out on all four sides over the loch and hills. It was simply furnished with a couple of oak settles, leather-covered armchairs, a large desk and a handsome Turkey red carpet. Above the desk was a large framed photograph of Silver Arrow. There was a telescope on a tripod trained upon the loch. The Lamberts were assembled when the three young people came in and Gray introduced them with a wave of his hand towards them. 'My assistants, Ian, Lesley and Frances.' And to them, 'Meet the Lamberts, Stu, Brett, Carrie and Sam.'

The Americans said 'Hi!' and the assistants murmured vaguely, then the buzz of conversation broke out again. Frances sought the seclusion of a deep window embrasure and from that vantage point tried to identify who was who. Stuart Lambert was undoubtedly 'Pop', as his offspring called him, a stout genial personage, very much the successful business man, but he had kind eyes, and made a point of addressing a few words to each of them. His wife, Caroline, was also plump, her opulent figure moulded by her foundation garment, expensively dressed and coiffured, her manner aggressive, as was that of her son Brett, a mean-faced man, whose eyes were too close together. His mother had spoiled him utterly, bringing him up to believe that anything he wanted he must have, by fair means or foul. Frances instinctively distrusted him.

The girl, Samantha, would have been pretty but for her petulant expression and slightly prominent front teeth. She had obviously tinted brassy hair, and hard blue eyes. She affected a nautical outfit, a sailor's blouse over wide navy slacks with a yachting cap perched jauntily on her curls. She called Gray 'darling' and touched him whenever opportunity offered. She gave both the other girls an appraising stare. Lesley she dismissed as negligible, Frances' good looks caused her a qualm, especially as Gray's eyes kept straying towards her, where she sat, a silent lavender-clad figure on the window seat, but she consoled herself by reflecting the girl was probably penniless while she herself was an heiress, and few men could resist the lure of wealth.

Murdoch handed round the trays of glasses with disapproval written all over him. He was a grizzled Highlander, who had served Gray since he was a boy and adored him.

After several whiskies, Brett began to boast.

'My old man's backing the wrong horse,' he declared. 'Silver Arrow hasn't a chance against my Sea Witch. All the wise guys are putting their dough on me.' He glanced at Gray and Frances sensed he hated and feared him, and he was not nearly as confident as he pretended.

'You're wasting your time competing,' he went on, 'and it'll cost you a packet to get your craft across the Atlantic.'

Gray smiled serenely. 'Your victory wouldn't be worth much if you had no serious competition.'

'And it's by no means a certainty,' Brett's father remarked.

A glance passed between the two, and Frances suspected that there was little sympathy between father and son and that was why Stu was sponsoring Gray. Brett weaved his way across to Frances, much to her dismay. He stood in front of her with a leer in his close set eyes.

'Some assistant!' he exclaimed. 'Sure Gray knows how to pick his dames, but you're wasted in this backwater.' His manner become confidential. 'Say, sister, why don't you come over to the States? That's a country fit to live in. I'd look after you, find you a job if you want one.'

Frances shrank from his bold gaze, which seemed to be undressing her.

'Thank you, but I'm quite content where I am,' she returned, aware that Gray was watching them with smouldering eyes. Evidently he did not approve of Brett's admiration, if it could be called that, but it was not her fault the young man had singled her out.

Brett sniggered. 'You another fan of his?' He

jerked his head towards Gray. 'Nothing doing for you there. Sam's got her hooks into him and she don't like competition, so hands off if you know what's good for you. But he isn't the only guy around. I'd be happy to console you.'

Gray made a movement towards them, but Sam put a restraining hand on his arm as she put a question to him.

Frances said coldly:

'You're under a misapprehension, Mr Lambert. I'm employed here, but not by Mr Crawford. His friendships are of no interest to me.'

But she was conscious of an ache in her heart. That brassy woman would not make a good wife and she was surprised Gray was attracted by her, but she was very rich and Gray was extravagant. She did not like to think that he could be mercenary-minded, but there had been a time when she would have denied furiously that Tony could be so, and she had been proved wrong, and she knew Gray less well than she had known Tony. If he were prepared to sell himself to the infatuated Miss Lambert, it was no concern of hers, and he was shrewd enough to know what to expect. Presumably he had counted the cost. She did not like these friends of Gray's, with the exception of the father, who seemed to be a good sort, and she wished he were not involved with them. Intuitively she was sure they would do him no good.

'You don't say?' Brett obviously did not believe her. 'But why so starchy? All these Misters! My name's Brett.'

Ian came to her rescue, distracting Brett with

some query about his speedboat, and imperceptibly
edged him away. Frances flashed him a grateful
look and caught Gray's baleful eye. She lifted her
head defiantly, as their glances locked. He had exposed her to the attentions of his obnoxious acquaintance and had no right to object to Ian's kindly
intervention. Samantha again took possession of him,
and soon after the party broke up.

Lesley was no more enamoured of the Lamberts
than was Frances, and as they descended the spiral
stair she said to her:

'That Brett's a nasty piece of work, and he'd do
Gray an injury if he could, while as for that bitch of
a girl . . .' She sighed. 'Pray God he keeps out of her
clutches!'

'I suppose it would be a good match for him?'
Frances asked tentatively.

'Good lord, no, he'd end by murdering her,
money or no money,' Lesley declared emphatically.
'Even if she loves him, and she's one who can only
love herself, he can't stand cloying women or suffer
fools gladly.'

Lesley's attitude towards Frances had changed
since her immersion in the loch, she was no longer
antagonistic, and now they were united by their
dislike of Samantha Lambert. Subconsciously they
were united also by their regard for Gray, but with
a difference. Lesley's feeling was obvious, but
Frances was unsure about hers. The man drew her
strongly and when he left he would leave a gap in
her life, but she was not in love with him, she assured herself almost feverishly. She would not let
herself fall in love with him; she had experienced

the pain of rejection once, and though Gray seemed to like her, he had no stronger feeling for her. Perhaps it was a good thing for her that he was going away, but she wished she could eliminate Samantha Lambert. She could sympathise now with the urge which had prompted Lesley to push her off the quay, it would give her immense satisfaction to do the same to Samantha, but being of a gentler disposition than Miss Ferguson, she was immediately ashamed of the thought. It might be Sam had a genuine affection for Gray, and her dislike was prompted by secret jealousy, which she could not justify. For she had no pretensions to have won Gray's love, it was presumptuous to even think of it. That kiss by the mere had only been a diversion to him. He had no doubt kissed Samantha too, and more wholeheartedly than he had her, if he were seriously thinking of marrying her. Frances went in to Margaret to give her an account of the party with a heavy heart.

CHAPTER FOUR

THE Lamberts left. Frances saw the luxury launch disappearing down the loch with a feeling of relief. At the conclusion of the party they had all drunk the healths of the competitors, and laughed about friendly rivalry. But Brett's laugh was forced and his eyes held a malignant gleam; there was no friendship there. Samantha had sighed and said coquettishly:

'I have to choose between my brother and my . . . boy-friend, so I'll hope for a draw.'

The pause before 'boy-friend' was noticeable; she had not quite dared to call Gray her fiancé.

Since Gray was still at Craig Dhu, Frances went every afternoon to the mere, hoping he might join her, but he did not appear. He was very busy finalising his preparations as his departure date drew near, but it was strange that he lingered by the loch, when his home town would have been more convenient. Lesley said it was to avoid his mother's lamentations, she being the worrying kind. The telephone in the office was always buzzing and Ian was sent daily into Mallaig to collect mail which otherwise might have been delayed.

On the third afternoon after the Lamberts' visit, Frances arrived at the mere and found Gray standing beside it, apparently waiting for her. It was a breezy day, with white clouds scudding over a blue sky, and not very warm. As usual when she caught sight of him unexpectedly, Frances' heart gave a lurch, and the gladness that welled up in her warned her that she was perilously near losing her heart to him, in spite of her determination not to do so.

'Too chilly to swim today,' he decided, and she felt disappointed, wondering why he had come if that were not his intention.

'Then I might as well go back,' she said despondently, but she made no move to do so. Caesar was standing beside him and she hoped he might suggest a walk.

He was fidgeting with the buckle of his belt—he

wore grey slacks and a blue tee-shirt—and seemed ill at ease. He kept looking at Frances searchingly and then away again as if he had something on his mind concerning her. She hoped he was not going to bring up the subject of Ian, recalling his inimical glances in their direction when the younger man had rescued her at the party. While he was away there would be no barrier to their intimacy, and he might be going to make some proviso concerning him, for he still seemed to be suspicious of their friendship, so much so that Frances hardly dared to speak to Ian in his presence. To her surprise he said suddenly:

'Let's go for a row on the loch.'

'That would be lovely, if you're sure you can spare the time.' She spoke demurely, but with a provocative gleam in her eyes. He had ignored her during the past few days.

His grey eyes crinkled amusedly.

'Been feeling neglected since I haven't met you here?'

She had, but she would die sooner than admit it. She had no claim upon his time and he had been very goodnatured to give her so much of it.

'Of course not. I know you've more important things to do, but I promised to practise regularly.'

'Do you always keep your promises, Fran?'

'If humanly possible.'

'Good, because I'm going to extract one from you which may be a severe test of your resolution.'

Ian, she thought despairingly. Have I got to swear I won't speak to him, or jeopardise my job? That lad's an obsession with him. How can I convince him that I only care for him as a friend?

But though she was sure of her feelings in that direction, she feared Ian's were very different. He never said anything, but his eyes were eloquent when he looked at her, and of course Gray had noticed. He was being tyrannical and unfair, for if she had returned Ian's devotion there was no barrier between them except possibly finance. She had no idea what the young man's prospects were, but presumably Gray could not debar him from marriage indefinitely, and he was himself involved with an American heiress, which should make him sympathetic. She resolved that if Gray made any unreasonable demand, she would speak her mind and risk dismissal. She did not think he would go that far now that she had made herself so useful to Mrs Ferguson, and she was not going to submit to his despotic whims, however much the others might kow-tow to him.

Although he was watching her face intently, Gray did not elucidate further. Instead he said suddenly:

'Race you down to the quay!'

His seriousness had vanished in a surge of boyish exuberance, and the trio set off down the hillside, Caesar barking excitedly. He outdistanced her easily, and when she reached the quay, out of breath and laughing, for the speed of her going had exhilarated her also, Gray was in the boat and shoving out an oar. Then she realised that this expedition had been premeditated, for the rowboat was not usually moored to the quay. There was even a cushion in the stern seat. He gave her a hand over the side, and Caesar followed cautiously; he was used to

boats and knew how to balance his bulk. Frances
seated herself in the stern and he curled up at her
feet, as Gray undid the painter and pushed the boat
away from the pier. It was an old rowboat, sturdily
built, with more strength than elegance. Apparently
the twins, whose names kept cropping up, used it for
picnics up the lake. Gray sculled easily, though boat
and passengers were no light weight. Frances wiped
her face with the towel she was still carrying, wishing she had her make-up with her; she had not put
any on for the anticipated swimming. Her hair hung
over her shoulders and she started to plait it.

'Leave it,' commanded the autocrat at the oars. 'I
like to see it flowing.'

'Anything to oblige,' she murmured with pretended meekness.

Gray rowed up the loch away from the sea. In
places the mountains rose steeply in rocky outcrops,
crevices in them filled with ferns and the ubiquitous
rhododendrons. Wild duck skittered across the bows,
occasional seagulls flapped overhead. Frances was
wearing a white dress with a mauve belted cardigan.
She was glad of the latter, for the wind was cold.
Her bare feet were encased in white sandals. She
looked down at them, remembering how Gray had
caressed them on the white sands of Morar. Unpredictable man, there was no knowing what he
would take into his head to do next, like this boat
trip today. A lump rose in her throat. Soon an ocean
would divide them, and how dreary the days would
seem without the excitement of his sudden appear-
ances.

Gray pulled into a little cove sheltered from the

wind, a miniature harbour. The prow of the boat grated on the shelving shore. He shipped the oars and sprang out to make the painter fast to a dead tree trunk, evidently put there for that purpose, and it must be a familiar spot, for Caesar jumped out, rocking the boat, and dashed away amid a flurry of wings from startled waterfowl. Gray climbed back into the boat and sat down on the plank seat facing Frances. Now it's coming, she thought, and she said lightly:

'Well, what is this serious promise you want me to make?'

He did not answer immediately, but absently fingered the rowlock. She noticed what beautiful hands he possessed, long-fingered, well shaped and sensitive. Then he threw back his head and looked straight at her.

'I want you to marry me, Fran.'

Had Caesar suddenly addressed her in human language, she could not have been more astonished. She stared blankly at the unrevealing features opposite to her. Gray looked as calm and unruffled as the summer sea.

'What . . . what did you say?'

'You heard. I need a wife, Fran. I'm thirty, already I'm past the average age for racers—racing in all its forms is a young man's sport. It's time I settled down and gave my energies to running the business. My father has a dicky heart, he might go any time, my brother-in-law is competent, he's managing director, but Alison, my sister, would like him to sell out, given half a chance. That I must prevent at any cost, Crawfords must go on. So when

I return from America I'm going to assume my responsibilities as head of the firm, but I don't want to live with my parents. I want my own home, and to make it a home, I need a wife.'

'I'm honoured,' she murmured vaguely, feeling bewildered.

He was actually proposing and he seemed to be in earnest, but what an unromantic way to go about it, as if he were setting out the terms of a business contract. There was no trace of emotion on his face, as if, as he had said, the acquisition of a wife was merely a necessary piece of furniture to complete his home. There had been more passion in him when he had kissed her by the mere, but she had not taken that seriously, and he had never hinted that he was contemplating such an important step. His indifferent attitude piqued her, and she added tartly:

'But why me? You hardly know me. Why not Lesley, or . . . or Miss Lambert?'

'Lesley is too temperamental, too young, she's like a kid sister. Sam . . .' He made a grimace of distaste. 'An egotistical fashion-plate. A man wants peace and comfort in his domestic life, and though our acquaintance has been short, I've watched you. You're blessedly serene and you don't flap easily. You know how to run a house.' He smiled faintly. 'I consider you're a treasure I shouldn't allow to slip through my fingers.'

This calculated assessment of her good points caused Frances to flush angrily.

'There's more to marriage than housekeeping,' she told him.

'Of course there is.' A glint came into his eyes,

and he grinned wickedly. 'We are ... physically compatible, which is very necessary.'

Frances' colour deepened and she turned away her head, trailing one hand over the side of the boat in the water, recalling their brief amorous encounters. Gray possessed the power to arouse her and she seemed able to ignite him, but she was no teenager to mistake sexual attraction for love, and that he had not mentioned. He did not love her at all, but had chosen her because he considered she was suitable for the position he had to offer her, a companion housekeeper with the bonus of mutual reciprocation in bed. At least he was honest; it would have been easy for him to woo her with false expressions of sentiments which he did not feel, but he preferred to be plainly, bluntly truthful. As she did not speak, he went on:

'From your point of view, it's quite a good proposition. You'd have a home and security, you can't want to be a home help longer than you must. You've no family, you told me, mine will accept you ...' he lifted his head proudly, '... as my choice. What about it?'

Indeed, what about it? To link her life permanently with this arrogant, overwhelming personality, who drew her strongly, even though she was slightly in awe of him. It was typical of him to suddenly decide to plunge into matrimony without any preliminary courtship—or did he consider the swimming lessons sufficient introduction? He had chosen her as the most congenial candidate to hand, and she could exonerate him from any mercenary motives, since she had nothing, and Samantha had so much, unless Sam had turned him down and this was the rebound, but from her own observations that was extremely unlikely. She was bewildered and excited by his offer, but as for accepting it, that required a lot of thought.

'You've mentioned an attachment to a fellow in Kent,' Gray continued, 'but I suspect he's a myth.'

'Oh no, he isn't, he's very real, but he preferred someone else.'

The admission caused her no pain. She had not thought of Tony at all during the past few weeks, and his image was becoming blurred. Gray was twice the man he was, and completely over-shadowed him.

'So you came up to Scotland to heal a broken heart?' Gray's tone was mocking. 'The surest way to do that is to put someone else in his place.'

'I'm not fickle,' she flashed, and wondered if she could be judged so for having got over Tony so quickly.

'Perhaps you weren't so deeply involved as you thought,' Gray suggested softly. 'One usually isn't.'

'Have you ever been in love?' she countered.

He shrugged his shoulders and smiled whimsically.

'Off and on, but we weren't discussing love,' he spoke the word with contempt, 'but marriage.'

Of which love should be a part, but Frances did not say it. Though she thought she had gauged his feelings correctly, she did not want to hear Gray say that love did not come into a marriage of convenience such as he was proposing. He was so much more experienced than she was, with only her modest little affair with Tony behind her, and was obviously scornful of the tender passion.

As she still did not speak, he told her:

'As well as everything else, I need the protection of a wife.'

Frances laughed at what seemed to her an absurd statement.

'You to need a woman's protection!'

'Oh, but I do. I hate to say it, but the more emancipated members of your sex are unscrupulous in the pursuit of their desires. I appreciate modesty in a woman, Fran, and you aren't blatant. I don't want to find myself compromised through some unpremeditated folly. I would never leave a girl in the lurch, however much she had herself to blame, and I'm fairly strongly sexed. You see the danger?'

Frances knew exactly what he meant, though she found his words distasteful. Women did pursue him and he was no Saint Anthony; if he made one pregnant he would feel he must right her. Frances admired his chivalry, rare in these days, though she did not appreciate his candour. She marvelled that a man who was supposed to be adept in erotic dalliance could approach her so bluntly. He might be paying her the compliment of complete frankness, but women liked a little camouflage. As if he guessed her thought, he said:

'I'm as good at concocting pretty speeches as any man, and I've uttered a lot of silly nonsense in my time, but I believe you're a sensible girl, Fran, and would prefer sincerity. If I declared I loved you to distraction and couldn't live without you, would you believe me?'

'No, I wouldn't,' she agreed, thinking how much she would like him to make such a declaration. Nothing could be less loverlike than the way he sat calmly facing her expounding practical reasons for their marriage. 'I would hate you to pretend what you don't feel.'

'Good. We understand each other.' He moved impatiently. 'Well, are you going to accept me?'

'I can't decide in five minutes,' she protested. 'You've taken me completely by surprise.'

'Have I?' He looked astonished. 'I don't generally waste a lot of time on a girl unless I have . . . intentions.'

So that had been the underlying motive for the swimming lessons, which she had put down to good nature. Used to feminine adulation, he would consider so many hours in his company would have made him irresistible, and she was ripe for an amorous proposition. That she would have understood and would have repulsed him firmly, but he had offered . . . marriage. He was right when he had pointed out that she had no future, unless she married. Domestic work was not exactly a career, and it would give her great satisfaction to ensure that the news filtered through to Tony that she had made a good match. But a loveless marriage whatever the material advantages was not ideal, and Gray had only obliquely mentioned love and that derisively, he did not seem to regard it as a necessary or important ingredient. He had decided he wanted a wife, and had chosen her because she had an even temperament, would make a good housekeeper and would be an undemanding mate.

Her own feelings towards him were mixed. Physically he attracted her strongly, but she had fought against it, not wishing to be one of a crowd. He had shown that he could arouse in her a passionate emotion which bore no resemblance to the tepid feeling she had had for Tony. It might be love or merely infatuation with a being so unlike anybody she had ever met before. She was vaguely aware that if he had loved her, he could awake in her a whole-hearted response, but he had made it very clear that he did not. He found her sufficiently desirable to be ready to sleep with her, and looked upon her as a sort of insurance against predatory females, and a pleasant companion to whom to return when he needed home comforts and relaxation. His absorbing interest was Silver Arrow and her success, next came the family business and she ran a poor third. Was it enough?

'I'll think about it while you're away,' she conceded. 'You may change your mind when you get to the States and everyone lionises you.'

'I can't wait,' he returned shortly. 'If I get a special licence there'll be just time to get married before I go.'

'Oh no!' This precipitancy startled and appalled her. But it was typical of the man who could never wait for anything he desired. 'That's much too soon!'

'What is there to wait for?' Gray looked away over the sparkling water. 'I might not come back.'

In the ensuing silence, a cloud passed across the sun, causing the bright scene to dim. Overhead a herring gull, planing on wide extended wings, uttered a melancholy croak. Frances shivered, drawing her cardigan more closely about her. Gray had always minimised the danger his sport entailed, but it existed. Anything that went at the speed of Silver Arrow presented considerable hazards. It was impossible to imagine that anyone so vital and virile as Gray could be extinguished, but it might happen.

'Don't go!' she cried impulsively.

'You're being ridiculous—of course I must go,' he reprimanded her. 'I've set my heart on Silver Arrow's triumph and I couldn't let Stu down. If the worst happens you'll be provided for as my widow.' He smiled sardonically. 'Others may claim to be ex-fiancées, but no one can dispute a marriage certificate.'

His thought for her touched her, though the implication shocked and chilled her.

'As if that mattered——' she began, and he interrupted her:

'It does matter. That's why we must be married before I go. I'll will everything to you, you'll acquire my holding in Crawfords—I'm the biggest shareholder—and it's up to you to keep the business going and prevent Sandy and Alison trying to sell. You'll do that for me?'

'Gray, for God's sake don't talk like that,' Frances exclaimed desperately. 'You'll be all right, you must be all right. And I haven't said I'll marry you.'

'But you will,' he insisted softly.

'I don't know . . . I can't decide . . .'

He leaned forward, staring at her intently. 'There isn't anyone else, is there?' he asked sharply, and his eyes glittered menacingly. 'You've not fallen for that besotted calf, Ian?'

He might not love her, but he could be jealous, and he had always resented her supposed fancy for his assistant.

'He isn't a besotted calf,' she declared indignantly.

'He appears so when he looks at you, and he is nearer your age.' His face contorted savagely: 'By God, I'll sack the pair of you!'

'Which would be ungenerous and unfair.'

His face changed. 'I suppose it would,' he admitted.

'There's no need for all this drama,' Frances said quietly. 'I can't help it if Ian fancies me, but as I've told you before, I've only friendship to give him.' She smiled shyly. 'He can't compare with you.'

Her clouded blue eyes met his gaze unflinchingly, and he laughed.

'I'm glad you've that much discernment. Then if there isn't anyone else, why the hesitation?' She turned her head away, and he went on persuasively: 'I'll be easier in my mind if I know your future is provided for. I hate to think of you wasting your youth waiting upon querulous old women, and freedom from worry is important to a racing driver. You wouldn't want to add to the risk, would you?'

She did not flatter herself that he would give her any thought once he had left the country and got among his racing clique, and she rather suspected that his concern for her was coloured by his desire to get his own way. Gray was ruthless in the face of opposition, and the role of benevolent father figure did not suit him, but his present anxiety might be genuine. She said insinuatingly:

'Do you really care what becomes of me?'

'Oh, for God's sake!' he exclaimed impatiently, 'haven't I made that clear?' A cunning gleam came into his eyes. 'Perhaps you'd prefer I fall a victim to Samantha's wiles?'

Frances did not think that a wife in England would be much of a deterrent to Samantha Lambert's advances if she were set upon capturing Gray, but at least he could not marry her. Perhaps that was at the back of his mind, for he knew Stuart Lambert would welcome him as a son-in-law, and he had already expressed his opinion of Sam. If pressure was brought to bear upon him, a wife at home would be a defence, though she could not imagine Gray allowing himself to be pushed into any situation against his will.

But the mention of Sam had a peculiar effect upon her, as possibly Gray had known it would. She had heartily disliked the American girl with her possessive attitude towards him, and to marry Gray would be to triumph over her. She had nothing to lose and a great deal to gain by yielding to him, so why quibble about the quality of his feelings? And love might come. She knew from that episode by the mere that they did, in modern parlance, turn each other on, which was something to build upon, if only it did not prove to be ephemeral. Nothing venture, nothing have, she told herself, and she said bravely:

'Very well, Gray, I'll marry you, and as soon as you please.'

She half expected a physical demonstration, but it

was not easy to embrace in a rowboat without
danger of overturning it, and all he said was, 'Sensible girl,' so that she had the feeling that he had
never been in doubt of her acceptance. She felt a
momentary surge of indignation against his arrogant
self-confidence, and suggested coolly:

'As it's more or less a marriage of convenience,
you're not proposing to ... er ... consummate it
before you go?'

She had spoken out of pique, and was unprepared
for the expression with which Gray greeted her
words. She had never seen naked desire on a man's
face before, but she saw it then, and her heart
turned over, but he masked it immediately.

'Where do you get these adolescent ideas from,
Fran?' he asked with a hint of steel behind the soft
drawl. 'Ever since that first night we met, I've
wanted to kiss you ... properly. Do you expect me
to deny myself when we may never meet again?'

Disturbed, she made no rejoinder, but turned
aside to again trail her hand in the water. Dimly she
realised that he knew the risk he was about to run,
and was eagerly snatching at every sensation, every
pleasure in case ... Because of that she could not
deny him. He watched her pensive face moodily for
some moments, then roused himself.

'Now where's that dratted dog?' He whistled.

It was some moments before Caesar appeared,
and they sat in silence, each busy with their
thoughts. Gray's gaze had gone to the distant moun-
tain crests, and Frances studied his face, wondering
to what she had committed herself. He was still
almost a stranger to her and there were depths in

him at which she could only guess. With her eyes upon the firm lines of his mouth, she decided he could, if provoked, be cruel as well as kind, and she hoped she would never encounter that side of his nature. At that moment he seemed to have gone away from her, and she surmised that his thoughts had fled to Silver Arrow. There was her real rival, a thing of steel and fibreglass, as opposed to flesh and blood. Absurd on the face of it, but only too true.

The sky became overcast and the waters of the loch heaved with warning of a storm to come. Gray whistled again, and at last Caesar appeared, galloping along the shore. He wagged an apologetic tail, as Gray heaved him aboard, and sat down with his head upon Frances' knees.

'We'll have him to live with us,' Gray decided, beginning to scull. 'You wouldn't mind?'

'No, I'd love to have him, but he takes up a lot of room.' She stroked the massive head. 'Unless he was kept outside.'

'No. A dog is a companion, not to be shut up like a wild animal. We'll accommodate him. We'll start house-hunting when I come back.'

Frances found these remarks reassuring, they gave substance to what had seemed a wild dream, but until Gray returned she would have to live somewhere, and she asked:

'Gray, need we tell the Fergusons? I'll have to go on living at Craig Dhu for a little while, until you come back, and it would be easier for me if they didn't know.'

He looked displeased. 'I meant to take you to my parents, it would be a more suitable arrangement.'

'But they would be strangers.' (And possibly antagonistic, not approving his choice.) 'It'll be an anxious time and I'd much rather be among people I
know and go on as if nothing had changed.'

'Something will have changed. You'll no longer
be a virgin.'

Frances flushed fierily as she met his sensual look
and he laughed.

'I like to make you blush, shows you've some red
blood in you. We'll spend a little time together after
the ceremony, but not at Craig Dhu. I'll arrange
something.'

Gray agreed, but with reluctance, to keep the
marriage secret until his return. Frances felt she
could not endure Lesley's venom and Ian's reproach
without his presence to support her, and it would be
worse being with his at present unknown parents.

By now the waves had increased and Gray was
having to pull hard to get the boat across the loch.
About half way over it started to rain. Frances
draped her towel over her shoulders, but it was not
much protection. Her hair streamed out on the wind
like a banner. The boat rose and fell with the surge,
but she was not afraid, storms always exhilarated
her, but by the time they reached the landing stage
she was soaked to the skin.

'Run up to the house and get dry while I put the
boat away,' Gray commanded.

As she ran Frances reflected that water seemed to
be the prevailing element in her life by the loch.
Later, soaking in a hot bath, she went over the
events of that incredible afternoon. She had promised to marry a man who had spoken no word of

love, and who on parting had not even kissed her, but had ordered her away peremptorily, as if he were glad to be rid of her.

CHAPTER FIVE

DURING the short period that was to elapse before Gray left, Frances went about her duties in a daze. The more she thought about it, the more fantastic the afternoon on the loch appeared. Surely she could not have been so mad as to promise to marry Gray? He was still almost a stranger, she had no idea what his tastes were or whether they had any interests in common. That did not seem to trouble him, and she rather suspected that his wife would be expected to take a back seat where his activities were concerned, which was contrary to the mutual reciprocation she believed was necessary to make a happy marriage.

Silver Arrow had been despatched in the charge of two mechanics from Crawfords; Gray was to follow by air, an arrangement which surprised Lesley and Ian. Ian expressed wonderment that Gray could bear to be parted from his precious boat even for a few days, but Lesley looked at Frances with speculative eyes. Frances feared she suspected there was something between her and Gray, for the girl was no fool and her love for Gray sharpened her perceptions where he was concerned. Gray had explained his delay upon the plea of important business still to be completed, and only Frances knew what that 'business' was. He did not seek her out and she was far too shy to venture to invade his privacy in the tower, and this lack of contact did little to combat her doubts. She was just beginning to believe his proposal was a fantasy, a product of her fevered imagination, when he waylaid her down by the quay, emerging from his office as she started for her afternoon walk.

'I've made all the arrangements,' he stated abruptly. 'We leave the day after tomorrow. You'll be ready?'

'Gray, I can't!' she gasped, as usual taken aback by his precipitancy, though she knew that if they were going to be married it must be immediately. So it was true, he had proposed and she had accepted him. 'What possible excuse can I give Mrs Ferguson for my absence?'

'I've thought of that. You'll tell her you've been invited to the funeral of a dear old friend. Thanks to our poor postal service, you've only just heard of her death. Margaret considers funerals are very important, that we should show respect for the dear departed, she won't keep you from your duty. You can tell her that you've already spoken to me and I've given you leave. Ian will bring you to Mallaig, where I'll meet you.'

He went on to give times and details as if he were discussing a journey in which he had no personal interest. Frances hated the deception he was forcing upon her, but it was her wish that the marriage should be kept a secret, so she had no right to complain about his ingenious scheme, but a funeral! She wished he had thought of any other pretext, it seemed ill-omened. She stood beside him gazing across the loch, unaware that despite his cool tones, his eyes were devouring her avidly. Then the overwhelming realisation that within a week he would be gone, and she would be left to face a future she was beginning to view with increasing misgiving, caused her to turn to him, her eyes wide and beseeching.

'Don't leave me, Gray. Take me with you. Why can't I come to the States with you?'

For a moment his gaze met hers, with a kindling flame, and she thought she had won. Then his face became impassive, and he said curtly:

'I'm afraid that's impossible, Fran. You can imagine the publicity if I turn up with a bride. "Speed ace's secret romance"—all that guff.' His lips curled with disgust. 'Besides, you'd spoil my concentration.'

Frances turned her head away, sensing she was outside his sporting life and he meant to keep her there. Like many men he divided his existence into watertight compartments. Silver Arrow was in one, herself in another, and never the twain should meet. He was going to devote three of his busy days to her honeymoon, and that he considered generous, but as for admitting her into a shared intimacy of his hopes and fears, that never occurred to him. He wanted her body, but was not interested in being a companion.

There was still time to draw back, but that she could not contemplate doing. Though Gray would not be brokenhearted, the rap to his vanity might disturb that all-important concentration, of which he had already spoken. Nor could she bring herself to break the tenuous bond between them. She was caught by the magnetism of his powerful personality, and she could not free herself from his spell, however much reason prompted rejection when he was not there.

Something of her disquiet communicated itself to him, as watching her pensive face, he said reproachfully:

'You promised, Fran; you won't go back on me?'

'No,' she answered firmly. 'I'll be there.'

She had accepted him upon his terms and she must abide by them and not repine for the love he could not give her.

He made a movement towards her and she looked up eagerly, but whether he had meant to embrace her was not to be known, for at that moment Lesley came out of the sheds and Gray turned away with a brief:

'So long, Fran, enjoy your walk.'

Aware of the other girl's suspicious glance, Frances smiled at her brightly and hurried away.

Mrs Ferguson grumbled when Frances made her request. It was short notice and the twins were due during those three days, a fact Frances had entirely overlooked, but of course she must pay her respects to her dead friend. Unfortunate that Kent was so far away and it would take a day to get there, and another to come back. Frances left her feeling a cheat and a hypocrite, but she had no alternative.

The next morning Ian took her into Mallaig. He would meet her there to bring her back. She was very pale with dark marks under her eyes, and he noticed it.

'Do you have to go, Fran? You don't look well, and funerals aren't exactly cheerful.'

'Oh, I must go,' she said quickly.

'Was she a very dear friend?'

For a second she looked blank, then declared hastily:

'Oh yes, she was,' and felt worse than ever.

She was in a state of mingled excitement and apprehension. She would not go back upon her word, but she knew she was pursuing a reckless course. That was stimulating, because she was not normally at all a reckless person, that and the incredible fact that Graham Crawford, speed ace, adulated by men and women of lesser breed, was going to marry her, and if the reasons he had given for doing so were not as romantic as she could wish, she would nevertheless be his wife.

Ian landed her at Mallaig with many injunctions to take care of herself. Gray had taken leave of the Fergusons the day before, saying he must say goodbye to his parents before going to the States. Lesley was tearful, Ian had been excited, confident of Silver Arrow's success. Gray had merely shaken Frances' hand, without speaking to her. So Ian had no idea that she was to meet him today, but she wondered how she was going to get rid of him, for he insisted on accompanying her to the station to carry her case. Then fortunately he had so many commissions to perform, he apologised for not waiting to see her depart, as he had so little time. As soon as he had gone, Frances hailed a taxi to take her to Morar. The sight of the white sands heartened her. Gray had been very kind to her on that memorable day—he could be kind upon occasion. She hoped he would be kind today.

She dismissed the taxi outside the small pub which was their rendezvous, and her heart lurched as she caught sight of Gray's car. He waited until the taxi was out of sight before he came to her. He was wearing a formal grey suit, very suitable for a bridegroom, and looked suave and elegant. Frances had dressed herself in a white dress and a blue linen coat. Lesley had remarked when she caught sight of her before she left that it would get very dirty on a train journey.

'So you've not failed me,' he said briefly.

'Did you think I would?'

He shrugged his shoulders. 'One can never be sure with women, but you're an honest girl, aren't you, Fran? I can always rely upon you.'

'Yes,' she replied, determined never to let him know how often she *had* nearly changed her mind. Now she was alone with him again, he had assumed his ascendancy over her and she wondered how she could have ever contemplated doing so. When she was seated in the car he produced from the locker a single white carnation arranged as a buttonhole with maidenhair fern.

'Let me pin it to your coat,' he requested. 'It's hardly a bouquet, but it gives you a bridal touch.'

She was pleased by this gesture and thanked him. As they drove away, she glanced out at the estuary where sunlight shone on the white sands.

'Morar,' she murmured dreamily. 'Where it all

began.'

When she had fallen under Gray's spell. She realised then that she was in love with him and it was
no use pretending she was not. Otherwise she would
never have consented to this marriage.

'What began?' he asked sharply. He seemed irrit-
able and on edge, and she hoped *he* was not having
second thoughts.

'I was thinking of that lovely day we spent together,' she explained, hoping he would reciprocate
by saying something tender. Gray frowned.

'Don't be sentimental!'

'But surely a bride can be allowed to feel sentimental on her wedding day?' she pleaded.

His response was deflating. 'Fran, I've suffered a
great deal from the mawkish outpourings of idiotic
females who should have had more regard for their
pride and dignity. From you I want sincerity, and
one of your attractions for me is that you don't
gush.'

Frances looked unseeingly out of the window at
the scenery. Gray's approach to this marriage was
entirely practical and materialistic, and it would
embarrass him if she confessed her love. He would
regard such a declaration as adolescent roman-
ticism. He did not love her, she was merely a women
he had selected because he considered her attributes
would make her the congenial wife he needed. The
only thing he really loved was Silver Arrow, and he
had expressed his contempt for emotional yearn-
ings.

Feeling snubbed and depressed, she did not speak
again during the drive to Fort William. As Ben

Nevis came in sight, like some great purple whale above Loch Linnhe, Gray remarked:

'You can come out of your sulks, we're nearly there.'

'I'm not sulking, but I don't want to be accused of gushing about the scenery,' she retorted. 'Sometimes you're a bit of a beast, Gray.'

'Sorry, darling, but I've a lot on my mind, so please bear with me. If I'm a beast, you're Beauty, and she redeemed the brute.'

This apology mollified her; it was the first time he had called her darling, but she feared she was the least of the things on his mind. She asked provocatively: 'Do you need to be redeemed, Gray?'

'This marriage is a step towards that.'

'I'm not sure what you mean by that, but I'd like to remind you I did suggest waiting until you came back and you'd less to think about.'

'And I told you I couldn't provide for you properly unless we were married,' he returned. 'Besides, I hate waiting.'

That was characteristic. She bit back a retort that she could always provide for herself; it was too late to draw back now, so there was no need to argue about an unlikely contingency. She prayed it was remote.

The register office ceremony with only themselves, the registrar and two witnesses was a dreary affair, and Gray said commiseratingly as they came out:

'I'm afraid I've defrauded you of all the trimmings so dear to a woman's heart, but my God, I couldn't endure the fuss of a big wedding, being on show to a lot of prurient spectators.'

'I don't mind about the trimmings,' Frances assured him, but she would have preferred a church service. She had not dared to suggest it, as she had no idea how he would react. There was so much about him she did not know, and suddenly she felt frightened. She had allied herself with a man who was almost a stranger for what were beginning to appear to be very inadequate reasons.

Gray had booked accommodation at an inn on the edge of Rannoch Moor for three nights in the names of Mr & Mrs Grey. It was a charming place, situated near the entrance to Glen Coe. Whitewashed, with three dormer windows in front, it stood beside a bridge spanning a stream of clear water. Behind it stretched the waste of the moor, fringed by distant mountains.

Lunch was served to them upon arrival in an oak-beamed room, but neither was hungry. Frances sat opposite to her new husband, very conscious of the gold band upon her finger. She flushed and paled every time she met Gray's glance.

'You're beautiful, Fran,' he said at one point, 'and untouched. Your male acquaintances must have been very unenterprising, luckily for me.'

Fleetingly she recalled Tony and his uninspiring kisses. He could never have moved her to want to anticipate marriage. Yet she had believed she loved him, but this new emotion which she felt for Gray might have led her into allowing him to seduce her if he had not offered marriage. She looked down at her plate to avoid the glitter in his eyes which made her heart flutter. She thought anxiously of the coming night, fearful she might be inadequate. She very much wanted to please him.

But Gray did not wait for the night. As Frances finished her coffee, he stood up.

'We'll go upstairs and ... er ... unpack,' he announced.

'That won't take long,' she said innocently, since they had only brought a couple of suitcases.

'Perhaps longer than you think.' He laid a possessive hand on her arm and propelled her from the room towards the stairs. Even then she did not divine his purpose, though he locked the door, and pulling off his coat, dropped it on the floor.

Frances, raised in near-poverty with a respect for care of clothes, picked it up, protesting:

'What a way to treat your beautiful suit!'

'Damn the suit!' he ejaculated. 'Put it down and come here.' He was ripping off his tie.

Understanding at last, Frances panicked. She dropped the jacket on a chair, and backed away from him.

'But, Gray ... not now ... it's too soon ... I didn't expect ...'

'Didn't you?' She shrank before the flame in his eyes. 'What did you think I brought you here for? A Sunday School outing?' He advanced upon her, his voice thickening. 'This morning you became my wife, and I have certain privileges.'

No love here, no tenderness, only an intensity of desire that would accept no denial. His cool and practical proposal had been no preparation for this upsurge of passion, nor had his matter-of-fact attitude throughout the day until now. He had scorned her suggestion of an unconsummated marriage, and she had anticipated they would sleep together, but not this brutal assault in broad daylight, for the hands that gripped her were not gentle and his kisses seemed to scorch her. He had pulled down her zip and her neck and bosom were exposed to his touch. But he schooled himself to stroke and caress her, using all his erotic skill to arouse in her the response he needed to ensure his own gratification. Slowly a dark tide of emotion rose and submerged her as he laid her upon the bed.

The sun moved towards the west, shafts of sunlight came through the window and illuminated the room in a golden glow. Frances gradually emerged from the traumatic experience which had shamed and bewildered her. All her shy sensitiveness, her natural reserve and virginal defences had been ruthlessly torn down and shattered. She knew she had clung to Gray in mindless rapture after the first painful moments, aroused to a pitch of sensual sensation of which she would never have believed herself to be capable, but now as her mind began to function again, she was shocked and shamed.

Hitherto, when she thought about it, the sex act had always represented the climax of love, a culmination of giving and receiving, sanctified by mutual love. But she knew very well that Gray did not love her, and what had passed between them, to her initiation, had to him been merely repetition of what he had often done before, his heart and mind had not been involved, only his senses. That she had been used made her feel degraded, that she had responded so eagerly humiliated her. He had been so arrogantly confident that he could conquer her, and that he had done so provoked a feeling of antagonism. She was a human being in her own right, not just an instrument to satisfy his lust. That she had lusts too was an unwelcome revelation.

Sounds from the bathroom indicated that Gray was having a shower, and when he emerged from it with only a towel wrapped around his middle, his fair hair dripping with water, Frances felt her pulses quicken at the sight of his beautiful bare body, which the slanted sunlight turned to gold and her resentment melted away. His physical ardour might be mistaken for love, but she was not deceived; what she feared was that so fierce a flame would burn out too quickly and then what would be left? As for herself, she was more than ever in love.

He sat down on the bed beside her, pulling back the cover which she had drawn over herself so that he could look at her recumbent figure. With a quick movement she swept it back again, throwing him a provocative look. He laughed.

'Still pretending to be shy? Mayn't I inspect my own property?'

Blue eyes challenged grey. 'You can rid yourself of that notion,' Frances told him. 'Women aren't possessions.'

'I might take you up on that, but there isn't time if we aren't to be late for dinner. Get up and dress, the water's hot if you'd like a bath.'

Baths ... dinner ... such mundane things when she was craving for some word of reassurance, a tender aftermath to his lovemaking. But Gray evidently had no such intention. He looked like a well-fed cat, as sleek and satisfied. One appetite appeased, he was thinking of his dinner. He stood up and stretched himself.

'I don't want any dinner,' Frances said, feeling peeved.

'Not mine host's fresh salmon?' His voice became plaintive. 'Am I to dine alone on my wedding night?'

'Oh, I'll come,' Frances cried contritely. She looked at him appealingly, wondering if she dared question him about his feelings for her. Now was the time he should say he loved her, even if he didn't. But he had turned away and was fiddling with the brushes on the dressing table, and looked as remote as Mars.

'Remind me to ring Stu tomorrow to check on Silver Arrow.'

So that was where his thoughts were straying; he could not forget the boat for a single day. Frances felt as though she had been plunged into cold water.

'Do you ever think of anything else?' she demanded tartly.

He smiled lazily. 'Sometimes.'

'Not often.' She sighed.

He said nothing to that, and coming back to her began to play with her long hair, drawing it through his fingers.

'I've always loved your hair, Fran, so fine and silky, it makes you . . . unique.'

Was that all that distinguished her from his other loves? She enquired timidly:

'You . . . you've had a lot of girls, Gray?'

He blinked. 'Be your age! What do you think I am? A monk?'

She said nothing, but her big eyes were sad.

Gray smiled quizzically. 'Believe me, Fran, you'd have had a rough time if I hadn't known my job.'

No, he was no ascetic and the technique he had used on her had been learned from other women, women who, poor fools, had probably loved him too, and where were they now? Her body excited him, but he took no interest in her mind or heart, any woman who caught his fancy could have served him equally well. But she was the one he had married, and that should comfort her.

They came down to dinner, for which Frances had put on a black lace dress she had bought for the occasion. Gray looked sleek and debonair in a velvet jacket and light-coloured trousers. She had never looked more lovely, she seemed to glow, and Gray watched her triumphantly, for he had brought that bloom to her beauty.

'At last you're alive, ice maiden,' he told her.

'Did you think I was a walking corpse?' she asked. 'Or a ghost haunting Craig Dhu?'

'No, only asleep. I knew I could wake you, though that clot Ian was trying to do so. But he didn't know how to go about it, I did.'

Frances did not want to think of Ian. He, she feared, did love her, and if she could have returned his love, they would have found the ideal for which she longed. *He* would not have been thinking of Silver Arrow directly after having made love to her.

He was a reliable, steady young man, without a yen for other girls, unlike this ... this faun, whom

she had been crazy enough to marry. To her relief
Gray changed the subject. His father's health was
deteriorating, he told her. As soon as he came back,
he must relieve him of his chairmanship of the company. This was much more congenial to Frances;
though she was sorry about Mr Crawford, whom she
had not yet met, Gray's statement gave a sense of
permanency to their relationship. He would not be
gone long, then they would find a house and settle
down to a normal existence. After all, many couples
married without love on both sides, and it worked
out all right.

'Tell me, Gray,' she asked shyly, 'do you want
children?'

He shrugged his shoulders. 'Not particularly, but
I suppose Crawfords should have an heir.' Then his
face lit up. 'If we had a son, he might be another
speed ace.'

Oh God, Frances thought, not that!

After dinner they took a stroll outside, watching
the last light lingering on the mountains. Frances
was feeling sleepy, and when she yawned, Gray told
her to go to bed and he would see her later. He
joined a group of fishermen in the bar, who had
dropped in for refreshment, and she went upstairs to
the sound of their raucous laughter feeling excluded.
She had hoped to beguile him into a really intimate
talk during which she might get to know him better,
but he preferred the company of other men, and
from the sound, their coarse jokes.

It was very late when he came to join her, and
she was asleep, but when he slid in beside her, she
awoke and wrapped her arms about him with pas-

sionate intensity. She had been dreaming and she had dreamed that she had lost him.

'Oh, Gray, I dreamed you'd gone . . .' she whispered.

'Well, I am going,' he returned prosaically, 'but I'll soon be back. Don't for God's sake start being hysterical, Fran.'

But he was gentler with her, less rapacious than he had been in the afternoon, and she was as hungry for him as he was for her. Finally they both slept, and she did not dream again.

Next morning Gray drove her down Glencoe, the scene of the hideous massacre of 1692, when the MacDonalds, men, women and children, were slain, a crime more reprehensible than others of the same sort, because it was a breach of hospitality, the men who committed it being the guests of the clan. The mountains enclosing it were too grim for beauty, particularly the stark humps of the Three Sisters, but it possessed a wild grandeur. Beyond the Glen, Loch Leven presented a kindlier appearance, reflecting the Pap of Glencoe which marked the entrance to it. Rhododendrons in full bloom coloured the landscape.

Gray drove down to Oban, the powerful car eating up the miles beside lochs and over hills. Arrived there, they had lunch, and then he insisted upon hiring a rowboat and taking Frances out into the bay, which was almost landlocked by the Island of Kerrera. He seemed consumed by nervous energy which would not let him rest. A suggestion from Frances that he should take things easy in view of the ordeal ahead of him was treated with scorn.

They left Oban after dinner, which Gray, made hungry by his exercise, ate hungrily, though Frances had little appetite. He seemed to be strung to a high pitch of tension, snatching at every satisfaction, as if . . . No, she must not think of that.

The sun was painting the sky over the Isles with gold, scarlet and purple as they left Oban; the sunsets there were famed. The colours were reflected in Loch Awe as the car swept by it, but over the Pass of Brandon, scene of many bitter conflicts, the shades of night were gathering. At Ballachulish a Scottish dance was in progress, and as the strains of the pipes reached them Gray stopped outside the hall and made Frances accompany him inside. A Highland fling was being performed, and after a poor attempt at it, Frances said she would prefer to watch. She had never done any Scottish dancing, and she was tired with her long day out. Gray sought another partner, after finding her a seat. She often forgot Gray was Scottish, but now, among his own kind, he became all Gael. Somebody lent him a kilt, to replace his trousers, and he flung himself wholeheartedly into the traditional dances with verve and skill. The fair-haired girl who partnered him when a partner was needed gazed at him with bedroom eyes, which did not seem to displease him. She whispered something to him, and he nodded. A space was cleared and crossed swords laid on it. Gray proceeded to execute the intricate steps of the sword dance amid loud applause. At its conclusion the floor filled again with upraised arms and whirling figures, who, as they became excited, uttered whoops and cries. To Frances, Gray had never appeared more alien; she had not seen this side of him, and she felt she had strayed into a foreign country and Gray was a stranger. He appeared to have forgotten her existence, and was returning the fair-haired girl's amorous glances with interest.

It was very late when they left and the stars gleamed brightly above Glencoe's sinister crags. Frances was weary and disgruntled, longing for the sanctuary of Gray's arms, but when they reached the bedroom he exclaimed:

'Damn it, I forgot all about calling Stu. Why didn't you remind me?'

'I forgot too,' she admitted. 'Was it important?'

'Yes, it was, I've had no news for two days.' He frowned at her. 'You're neglecting your wifely duties, Fran.'

Stung by his tone, she retorted:

'I didn't know they included acting as a memo pad. You were too occupied with that yellow-haired girl to welcome a reminder.'

His grey eyes narrowed to slits.

'I can't abide jealous women, Fran,' he warned her.

'I wasn't jealous, only neglected.'

'But you didn't know the dances . . .'

'I'm English, reels and flings were not included in my education.'

'Then you'd better accustom yourself to being a Scottish wife.'

He looked menacing, and Frances knew they were perilously near a row, and over such a trivial matter. With an effort she conquered her resentment.

'It's not too late to make your call now, there's a time lag . . .'

'Fancy knowing that!' he gibed.

'It's a well-known fact . . .'

'But I thought you resented anything to do with the States and Silver Arrow.'

So he had sensed her antagonism to his speedboat, though she had tried to conceal it. Ignoring his remark, she suggested he had better ask for his call before it got any later.

'Probably take half the night getting a connection,' he grumbled. 'I'll say goodnight, Fran, you'll be asleep by the time I'm through.'

The implication was obvious; he did not intend to make love to her tonight. Stuart Lambert, or more correctly Silver Arrow, had impinged upon her honeymoon. Wearily she undressed and got into bed. She should not have mentioned the fair-haired girl, but after all, she was only to have three nights with Gray and already Silver Arrow and a stranger had encroached upon them. With difficulty she restrained her tears; it would never do for Gray to discover a wet pillow. What time he came up she had no idea, for, exhausted, she fell into a deep sleep, and when she awoke in the morning, only the impress of his head beside her and the general untidiness of the room indicated that he had been up at all. She went to bathe in some distress; already Gray seemed to have tired of her. He might be more attentive when Silver Arrow had won her race, but she doubted it. There seemed to be no prospect of ever winning his love.

He came in to eat an enormous breakfast, telling

her he had tramped all over the moor, and how much he had missed Caesar. His dog, Frances noted, not his wife. She asked:

'Why didn't you wake me? I'd have come too.'

'You were so sound asleep. I didn't want to disturb you.'

He went on to say he must go to Glasgow to say goodbye to his parents.

'But I thought you'd done that!' Frances was dismayed.

'I was too busy making the arrangements for our wedding and whatnot.' He noticed her expression. 'You can come with me if you like. You'll have to meet them some time.'

But not now, on the eve of his departure, and he did not sound as if he wanted her company.

'I think I'd better wait until your return,' she told him. 'Bit trying for them to have me foisted on them when they'll want to give all their attention to you.'

He shot her a keen glance, seemed about to protest, then shrugged his shoulders. 'As you please,' he said indifferently. 'I'll be back in time for dinner.'

It was a grey day, wreaths of mist encircling the hills. The skies seemed to be weeping. Frances decided it was the weather that made her feel so despondent as she walked beside the stream. Naturally Gray wanted to see his parents, especially as his father's health was precarious and she had been mistaken when she thought he had already taken his leave. She must not expect too much from him, he had never pretended that he loved her. He would only be gone a couple of weeks, Stuart had wanted him to stay a while after the race, and she must concentrate upon making their life together a success upon his return. They would create their home in a calmer atmosphere than during these hectic honeymoon days, and she must ensure it really was a home. He appreciated her serenity and she must stay unruffled whatever the provocation, and in time she might win his love, make him realise Frances née Desmond was a person not merely an instrument to slake desire. The physical reciprocity between them was not to be despised, but passion was too ephemeral to make a solid basis to their life together, they needed more than that.

She did not think Gray would find it easy to settle down to a conventional life, and it would be her task to help him with her love and understanding. She knew now that she loved him devotedly; he had mastered not only her body but her entire being. Surely love as strong and deep as hers must reach him eventually?

Gray was late for dinner and Frances met him with no word of reproach for his day-long desertion but listened patiently to his enthusiasm about the publicity that he had found had been built up around Silver Arrow. She was the favourite to win. His boat was in the ascendant now, he could talk of nothing else, and he did not seem to see her when he looked at her. Stu was already at Miami and was looking forward to his coming. She could not help asking:

'Will Miss Lambert also be there?'

'Sam? Oh, she'll be somewhere around.'

His complete indifference reassured her. But that night her fears and uncertainties returned in force, all the more potent because they were intangible. She clung to him with such desperate intensity that he was surprised.

'Darling, I'm not going away for ever. I know it's a deprivation for . . . both of us, but it won't be for long.'

She noticed the tiny pause before the 'both'; he would not be deprived, already he had gone from her in spirit, and tears rose in her eyes.

'Don't turn into a weeping Niobe,' he chided her, as a tear splashed on his chest. 'Brave women send their men into battle with smiles.'

And so she smiled until her lips were stiff, all through breakfast, and during their goodbyes. Gray was leaving for the airport, and a taxi was calling for her to take her to Mallaig. His final embrace was perfunctory, as he said lightly:

'When I come back I'll crown you with my victor's laurels.'

It was another grey day, and Frances watched his car disappear into the grey murk with a sense of foreboding. Suppose Silver Arrow did not win, suppose . . . no, she must not think of that. But there was another possibility—suppose among the bevy of American fans, all more sophisticated and smarter than herself, he came to regret his hasty marriage? There would be wealthy women who could help Crawfords financially, which she could not, and divorce was easy. Her hold over Gray was so slight, it could be broken without much difficulty or even regret on his part. He was the love of her life, but to him she was only another woman with whom for expediency's sake he had forged a bond, that had no great binding force.

The mist began to roll up the mountainsides that guarded the entrance to Glencoe, the Glen of Weeping, as it was called. The sun broke through the mist, a happy augury, surely. But Frances could not wholly free herself from her depression, the conviction that for one reason or another she had looked her last upon Graham Crawford. I'm being morbid, she told herself; it's this place, I'll be better when I get back to Craig Dhu.

A car pulled up in front of the inn, and the driver got out, enquiring for Mrs Grey, which was the name under which Gray had registered. With a start she realised he meant herself and went to collect her case.

In the car she surreptitiously slipped off her wedding ring. She was Miss Desmond again until Gray came back to claim her.

CHAPTER SIX

THOUGH Gray was supposed to be away for only a fortnight, the Fergusons did not expect him back at the end of that time. His movements were always erratic, and he might decide to go off somewhere else, though in view of his father's illness he should return unless Mr Crawford made a complete recovery. Only Frances knew he had another reason for coming back promptly, and she was confident he would not let her down; moreover, he had promised that this was to be his last fling, before he settled in to the company routine.

It was not until Frances was back at Craig Dhu that she remembered they had made no arrangement about telephoning or correspondence. A letter would probably arrive about the time Gray would, but she was sure he would ring her, and she hoped he would remember to use her maiden name if alternatively he wired her. She desperately longed for some message from him, though she feared he might not understand her need. The three days on Rannoch Moor had a dreamlike quality, and as she slipped back into her normal duties, it was difficult to credit that they had actually occurred. Only at night when her newly awakened senses craved for him, she knew they most definitely had, for he had broken through her virginal inhibitions and left her a yearning wife. She was restless and apprehensive, her consolation being that each unhappy night brought their reunion a day nearer.

Gray had been entered for other offshore events, but the Miami–Nassau race from the U.S. to the Bahamas was the important one. If he were among the first six finishers, he would be eligible for a world championship as ruled by the Union of International Motorboat Racing, for he had already achieved the necessary number of points in two other international events as laid down as compulsory by it. That was his ambition to win before he retired. Lesley scoffed at the idea of his intended retirement, of which he had made no secret.

'It's in his blood,' she declared, 'He'll never give up unless he becomes crippled or is beaten hollow, and that he'll never be.'

Frances was much afraid she might be right.

She was kept too busy during the day to have much time for brooding. The twins, Jo and Jac, abbreviations of their baptismal names of Josephine and Jacqueline, which they detested, made a lot more work, particularly in the preparation of meals. They were lively teenagers, very similar in appearance, with mops of reddish curls and greenish eyes like their elder sister's. Frances was thankful for the diversion they created, which gave little opportunity for Margaret to question her about the funeral, in which she showed a morbid curiosity, and Frances hated to have to tell lies. Lesley had greeted her with probing glances which seemed to question its genuineness, but she did not say anything, for there was little time for private conversation with either Jo or Jac barging in upon them, demanding this and that. They had inspected Frances with critical looks and sighed with relief, which they later explained ,.

'When we heard Mum had got a help, we expected an old fuddy-duddy who'd disapprove of us,' Jo told her candidly, when they were helping Frances with the supper wash up. 'But you're not old at all.'

'And quite good-looking,' Jac conceded. She giggled. 'I believe my brother's sweet on you.'

'Nonsense,' Frances returned quickly. 'We're just good friends.'

'Says you, but of course you've got a crush on Gray, like we all have, though none of us have a hope with him.' She sighed. 'Bet he's having a whale of a time with those glam American girls!'

'Ian thinks Sam Lambert's after him,' Jo said mournfully. 'Suppose he comes back married?'

Jac laughed scornfully. 'Married? Our Gray? Hoots, lass, he'll never wed, he likes to play the field.' She became serious. 'Of course it would be a good thing for Crawfords if he did marry Sam, she's loaded, and the firm needs some capital investment.'

Not enjoying this conversation, Frances pointed out that it was a lovely evening and if they wanted to make the most of the last of the daylight, they had better go out, and they scampered off. Left alone, Frances completed the last of her chores in a mood of depression. Gray had said one of his reasons for marrying her had been to ward off predatory women like Samantha, but she thought he had been joking. She wondered if what the twins had said about Crawfords were true, and whether Gray would regret the opportunity he had missed by marrying her, when he thought about it. He took a lively interest in the business. He was not enamoured of Samantha, but then he had not married herself for love, and if expediency pointed to Sam, what then? She had an idea divorce in the States could be easy and swift, in Reno or some such place. Then she shook herself mentally. If she could not trust Gray for a fortnight, it was a poor lookout for their future.

Speedboat racing has not a great appeal in Britain, it is too expensive and exclusive a sport to compete with football or tennis. So there was little reportage in the British press, but one paper did print a photograph of Gray after winning a minor event, with Sam putting what looked like a Hawaiian lei about his neck. The caption said: 'Playgirl Samantha Lambert rewards British speed ace Graham Crawford. Is there a romance in the offing?'

Lesley showed it to Frances with a malicious gleam in her eyes, as if she were issuing a warning. Frances made no comment.

Since there was no television at Craig Dhu, Ian and Murdoch spent the day of the race fiddling with the radio in Gray's tower, to be sure they could tune in to get the result. Owing to the difference in time they would not hear until the late evening. They refused help and advice from the twins and told the rest of the household to keep out. They would inform them as soon as there was anything to report.

Frances had had no word from Gray, though they had all wired messages of good luck the night before. She supposed she was expecting too much. Gray would be living in a whirl of activity, but he might have remembered, she thought resentfully, that he had a wife. A nasty niggling doubt assailed her. Perhaps he had forgotten! She was not all that important to him, and he was absorbed in that other part of his life to which he had never admitted her. She began to wish she had not insisted upon keeping their marriage secret. It was galling to be treated like an outsider, when she was nearest to him of all, for the Fergusons were not even related to him. But she could not face the surprise and disbelief a revelation would cause if she made it now. Gray had taken charge of their marriage certificate and she might have to get a copy to convince them. It was not worth all the fuss when Gray would be back so soon. She had her ring, which she put on at night, it being a link with him who had put it on her finger. Forsaking all other ... but Gray would never forsake Silver Arrow for her, and the boat had claimed him.

They all congregated in the sitting room after an early supper, waiting for Ian to bring them the news. Margaret Ferguson, who was the least involved, made desultory conversation. Even the twins were quiet, while Frances was rigid with suspense. In her mind's eye she saw Silver Arrow as she had first seen her, sweeping up the loch in a cloud of spray. She looked at the clock; it would be finishing now, the end of that long trek through blue waters. Over there it would be still afternoon. The minutes ticked remorselessly on. Surely Ian would have got the announcement by now? Perhaps he couldn't get through and they would have to wait until morning for news. They heard him coming downstairs, slowly, heavily, and as he came in he met their anxious eyes with a shake of his head.

'She didn't win?' Lesley asked flatly, while Frances' heart seemed to stop beating.

'Silver Arrow was out of the race,' Ian told them. 'A mechanical fault—she had to be withdrawn.'

They looked from one to the other with dismay, and Margaret remarked with irritating casualness:

'Machines always go wrong when most needed ...'

Her children gave her murderous glances.

'Who did win?' Jac enquired.

'Brett Lambert's Sea Witch gained the most points.'

Lesley sprang to her feet, her green eyes flashing.

'Damn him, damn him!' she cried furiously. 'I'm

sure he had something to do with it. He didn't want Silver Arrow to win. Oh, I could kill him!'

'Lesley, what language!' her mother reproved her. 'The Lamberts were his hosts. You shouldn't say things like that, even if you are upset.'

'The security guards wouldn't let anyone near the speedboats,' Ian pointed out. 'Perhaps she was injured in one of the other races, or on the journey over.'

'Gray shouldn't have let her out of his sight,' Lesley declared. 'He should have gone with her, she might have been tampered with before he came, and the damage only became apparent before the big race.'

'Gray made all the arrangements,' Frances said dully.

'Of course he did,' Mrs Ferguson intervened. 'He knew best. What did the broadcast say about Gray, Ian?'

Ian sighed heavily. 'He wasn't mentioned.'

'It'll break him!' Lesley stormed. 'He'd set his heart upon success. Someone has been criminally negligent. Silver Arrow was in perfect condition when she left.' She clenched her fists. 'Sabotage!' she hissed.

'Now, Les, don't make wild statements,' Margaret told her. 'You never know where you are with machinery.'

'It's reliable enough if it's properly checked and maintained.'

'I'll get through to the Crawfords in the morning,' Ian interposed. 'They may have heard from Gray.'

Frances felt a jealous pang, it was she he should

contact, not them. 'I'll crown you with my laurels,' rang in her ears, but there would not be any laurels. Her heart bled for her husband. She did not know him well enough to anticipate his reaction. He would be disappointed, but he was a proud man and would resent condolences. She longed to be with him to comfort him, but would he accept her sympathy? He was so very much the arrogant male, he might reject it. If he had loved her, he might have turned to her; love could give solace and healing without offence or injury to pride, but he would take any form of pity as an affront to his manhood. Though legally she was his nearest and dearest, he did not see her in that light, and if he went to anyone it would be his mother, she thought bitterly.

There was no hope of any more news that night, and with the exception of Mrs Ferguson who would never allow anything to do with motorboats disturb her, none of them slept much. Even the twins, who usually went out like a light, were restless. As for Frances, she did not try to sleep. She sat by her window gazing out at the dark loch. It was a still night, spangled with stars, and she thought how indifferent nature was to their puny human woes. The stark hills and quiet water had watched so many dramas of life and death through the passing years. War and pillage, fire and slaughter had been frequent occurrences in the days gone by, but new grass covered the blood-soaked earth, and fresh generations replaced the slain, while the hills remained the same, only an occasional flood or landslide disturbing their tranquillity.

Gray was alive, there had been no accident to

Silver Arrow endangering his life, only his pride and ambition would suffer. By the time he returned he would have recovered from the worst of his disappointment; he was too much of a man to be wrecked by failure. They had all the future before them, and he had said he was going to devote himself to the business and they were to have their own home. He would have plenty of diversions to distract him from Silver Arrow's incomprehensible mechanical fault, and there would be some stormy inquests in the shipyard where she had been built. But though her shadow would fall on him for some time to come, she was after all only an expensive toy, and his racing a hobby, which he had already decided to give up. Frances decided she must encourage him to look forward and forget what might have been.

By the time the early dawn light crept over the mountains, Frances had reasoned herself into a more optimistic state of mind. She was able to sleep for a couple of hours before facing the new day, but at the back of her mind was an uneasy presentiment that Gray was not going to be as conformable as she hoped.

Next morning there was a paragraph in the paper about the event, but it merely gave the times and points won by the leading boats. It stated that many people were disappointed by the withdrawal of Graham Crawford's favoured Silver Arrow, but that was all. No mention of what was wrong with her.

'You'd think there must have been someone there who could have repaired her,' Ian observed, frowning at the paper. 'And I know we supplied plenty of spare parts.'

Lesley pushed away her uneaten breakfast. 'I tell you there's more in this than has been reported.' She was very greatly upset, for she had taken as great a pride in Silver Arrow as Gray had done.

Ian's call to the Crawford home got no reply, but upon contacting Sandy McIntosh, Gray's brother-in-law, he was told Robert Crawford had had a severe heart attack and was in intensive care in hospital, and his wife was with him. He had wired the news to Gray who would of course come home at once. Misfortunes never came singly, Frances thought—first the débâcle over Silver Arrow, and now this. She knew such a collapse was not un-expected, but it would be a sad homecoming for Gray. But he would come, might be on his way that very moment. She felt her pulses stir, there would be no need for further concealment. She would assume her correct status as his wife. However inadequate she might be, he would claim her and in the inti-macy of bed she might be able to reach him, give him the comfort he would so sorely need.

Days passed, and Gray did not come.

Ian was impatient for the return of Silver Arrow, so they could check what had gone wrong. He went down to the Glasgow works, but they had not been advised of her despatch. He called at the Crawford house, where he saw Alison. Her father was still on the danger list, she told him, and her mother was resting. They had heard nothing from her brother and Gray was a swine; she was very indignant, not to have at least communicated with them. When this news was relaid to Frances, she realised Gray had not told his family about his marriage, nor did it

seem an appropriate time to reveal it. She wondered
if something could have happened to him, but if so
his people would have been advised, for presumably
he was still staying with the Lamberts. The twins
suggested he was remaining in America to take part
in some outstanding event to vindicate Silver Arrow,
but that was very unlikely and did not account for
his silence.

Frances had a different idea: Samantha. Had he
succumbed to her blandishments or been so dazzled
by her wealth, he was deliberately keeping away
because he meant to break up their marriage? The
thought tormented her, in her misery and suspense,
though it again was improbable. Even for Sam he
would not keep away while his father was dying, or
would he? She knew only too well he could be
carried away by the desire of the moment, as he had
rushed into marrying her. She grew thin and pale,
but not even Ian remarked it, he had too much else
to occupy him. For Robert Crawford died, and with
Gray incommunicado, all their futures were in jeop-
ardy. Ian and Lesley went to the funeral, fully expecting to meet Gray there. Frances felt her exclusion bitterly, but her duties kept her at Craig Dhu,
and without disclosing her secret, she had no excuse
to go. But if Gray was there, surely he would return
with the Fergusons to claim her? She spent the day
in a fever of anticipation, but they came back with
doleful looks. No one had heard from Gray.

A week later, Sandy McIntosh came to Craig
Dhu. He was a very ordinary-looking man, brown
hair thinning on his scalp, shrewd dark eyes. He
wore an impeccable business suit and carried a brief

case, all that was required to complete the picture of a City gent was a bowler hat and an umbrella. He was the antithesis of Gray. He was Scottish and dour and firmly refused to discuss business over the lunch Frances had cooked. He was going back the same night. After the meal, the twins were sent outside, and when Frances brought coffee to them in the sitting room, she seated herself in the window behind the curtain hoping she would not be noticed. She wanted desperately to hear what he had to say.

'Weel, since I couldna win word nor writ from Graham, I flew over to the States to call on that mon Lambert. Gray wasna theer, and Lambert didna ken where he be.'

He paused to let his words sink in. 'He's disappeared.'

'But . . . but why?' Ian queried.

Sandy shrugged his shoulders.

'My brither-in-law has always been irresponsible, thinking Crawfords only existed to build his speed-boats. Maybe when his hopes were dashed, he took off for Alaska or China, I wouldna put it past him. He'd plenty of funds because he'd sold that boat of his.'

'Sold Silver Arrow!' Lesley exclaimed. 'He'd never bear to part with her.'

Sandy frowned at her. 'Forbye, he has.'

Ian said slowly: 'Gray would have no use for a machine that had let him down, or ever forgive a person who betrayed him.'

Frances felt a cold trickle down her spine. Was Gray really so implacable? But she would never give him cause to turn against her.

'That lass of Lambert's was making a reet to-do. Said Graham was her fiancé and he'd left her flat.'

So he had not told Samantha he was married, contradicting his declaration that he needed the protection of a wife, not that Frances had ever taken that statement seriously. What had he said to her to lead her to suppose they were engaged? She heard Sandy's next words through a blur of pain. He was stating that Gray's disappearance and Robert's death had left the company in difficulties. They would have to economise. The Fergusons would have to return to Glasgow immediately, and Craig Dhu must be sold. The place had always been a white elephant, another of Gray's little extravagances. Murdoch and Morag could be pensioned off. His eyes fell on Caesar, stretched on the hearthrug.

'And yon's yet another. That braw great beastie will have to be put down if we canna find a home for him.'

'Oh, no!' Frances cried, pushing back the curtain. 'Not Caesar—Gray loves him.' The dog, hearing his name, got up and came to her, laying his head on her knee. 'Gray would never forgive you if he comes back and finds him gone.'

'*If* he comes back, but who may you be?'

His wife, trembled on her lips, but Ian forestalled her, explaining her position.

Sandy looked even more dour, for he had noticed she had used Gray's first name, a familiarity he did not approve of from a 'help'.

'I'm thinking ye'll be out of a job, miss.' He stood up, preparing to depart. 'Ah weel, I'll bide a while, but if Graham doesna show up soon, it must be as I said. Firm's running at a loss.' He stroked his thinning hair. 'Just like that lunatic to run out on us when his father's dead!'

'But he didn't know about that,' Ian defended the absent one.

'He left no address,' Sandy snapped. 'Lambert's going to ask the police to try to trace him, so maybe we'll hear something soon. But he's no kin of yours, and you'd best be looking out for yourselves.'

But he was of hers. Frances looked from one to the other of their dismayed faces and wondered if she dared proclaim herself. Gray had given as another reason for their marriage, that she would be provided for, but there did not look as though there was going to be much provision, and that was in case he was killed. But she was not his widow, merely a deserted wife, which put her in a different category, nor could she believe Gray would not return in spite of Sandy's aspersions. Possibly the damage to Silver Arrow had unbalanced him temporarily, though it was difficult for her to credit that even the defection of Silver Arrow could so affect him. She decided she would do as Sandy was going to do, bide a while and continue to hope to hear from him. The reference to Samantha had disturbed her, all along she had suspected she was at the bottom of his delay. She was making a 'reet to-do', but that might be camouflage and she did know where he was. To those who love deeply, jealousy is an ever-present bugbear, and Frances had no great opinion of her own attractions. Samantha had a great deal to offer, and she so little.

The twins put forward impossible suggestions. He

had been kidnapped—but no one had asked for a ransom. He had eloped with a fabulous glam girl—that from Jac, and Jo scoffed. He might, she said, be prospecting for gold to finance Crawfords. No one suggested he might have been murdered, that was a possibility they could not face.

As the days passed, Frances had another pre-occupation. She often felt queasy in the mornings, and when a month had gone by, she suspected her honeymoon was to have an aftermath. Much as she would like to have a child, the circumstances were not propitious. She was alone in a strange country with no friends, except perhaps Ian, and to him she dared not turn, knowing how Gray would interpret any intimacy between them. She had never before felt so lonely and bereft, more so than when her mother had died and she had lost Tony. Again she became aware that Lesley was watching her—nothing seemed to escape those sharp green eyes. She, Frances, counted as an enemy, and she was the last person in whom she would want to confide.

One morning, Frances was overcome with nausea at the breakfast table, and hastily retreated to her room. She had not been up there long when there was a tap upon the door. Frances made no response, hoping whoever it was would go away, but the door was pushed open and Lesley walked in.

'Go away,' Frances bade her, 'I don't feel well and I want to be alone.'

Lesley seated herself upon the unmade bed and regarded her calmly, Frances was pale and distraught.

'You're going to have a kid, aren't you?' she said

bluntly.

It was still too soon to be sure, and Frances returned Lesley's cool green gaze with a touch of defiance.

'What makes you think that?'

Lesley smiled faintly. 'Bravado won't get you anywhere, Fran. It's Gray's, isn't it?'

Frances hesitated. If her pregnancy were confirmed, she would have to reveal her marriage, though she shrank from the inquisition that would follow. Lesley had come to gloat over her, the fallen woman, deserted by her lover and carrying the fruit of her shame—the melodramatic phrases filtered through her mind. But Lesley was not going to have that triumph; her baby would not be illegitimate.

'I'd be obliged if you'd mind your own business,' she said coldly.

'Your child's going to be a lot of people's business,' Lesley retorted. 'Oh, I know you went off with Gray—only Mother was dim enough to believe in that bogus funeral. You looked quite different when you came back. Sort of glowing.' Her pointed face became wistful. 'Fulfilment, I suppose.'

'You're very observant,' Frances said drily. She lifted her head proudly. 'We were married.'

'Why, of course, Gray's not a heel,' Lesley declared, to Frances' astonishment. 'I know he goes bullheaded for what he wants, but he'd never seduce you and leave you in the lurch.' She got up and began to pace the room. 'I've never known Gray so infatuated with a woman—a good woman. Usually he goes with floosies for kicks, who are only out for a bit of fun, so no one's hurt.' She stopped and stared at Frances. 'I know what took his fancy, you've got an out-of-this-world look at times, which men always find a challenge. They're all hunters, you know, and attracted by shy game. Most of Gray's women hunted him, which he doesn't appreciate.' She grinned impishly. 'But he's brought you down to earth with a bump, hasn't he?'

'I daresay your theories are very interesting,' Frances said stiffly, a little puzzled by the other girl's attitude. 'I know you've always hated me . . .'

'I did,' Lesley cut in. 'You'd got what I wanted, and could never have, and you didn't seem to value it, though I'm sorry I pushed you in the loch. It was a crazy impulse and I've felt awful about it ever since. Can you forgive me?'

'I . . . I'd almost forgotten about it.' She had, it seemed so long ago. 'I never meant to take him from you . . .'

'He was never mine,' Lesley said bitterly. She shrugged her shoulders. 'These things happen, we have to endure them.'

'Of course I'll go away,' Frances told her, though she had made no plans as yet. 'You won't have to put up with me.'

'Where will you go?'

'Oh, somewhere.' Frances moved her hands vaguely. Her future looked horribly bleak. She could appeal to Gray's mother for help, but she wished she need not do so. Could she possibly manage somehow . . . alone?

'Don't be a fool,' Lesley said scornfully. 'You must take your rightful place as Gray's wife.'

'But . . . but his family doesn't know me. If they're

all like Mr McIntosh, who was conventionality personified, they'll be shocked, feel Gray's made a mesalliance . . .' She covered her face with her hands. She had wanted to keep her romance inviolate, a beautiful, private memory; now the whole thing would be dragged into the light of day, to be criticised, condemned, even ridiculed. 'I can't bear it!'

'You won't have to bear anything, except your kid,' Lesley told her. 'From now on, I'm going to look after you, see you get your rights, because I'm sure you're a poor hand at looking after yourself.'

Frances gaped at her. 'But . . . why?'

'Oh, I suppose partly for Gray, and partly for you.' She laughed. 'You rouse my protective instincts, and until Gray comes, I'll be your bulwark.' She looked away. 'He might thank me.'

'Much he cares,' Frances cried bitterly, recalling the long, lonely nights during which she had ached for him. 'He takes all a woman has to give and goes his own selfish way.' She clenched her hands. 'Sometimes I feel I hate him!'

For if he had left her alone, she would never have been awakened to this desperate need of him which tortured her, this soul-searing unrequited love.

'I've often hated him,' Lesley said calmly, 'but I've never stopped loving him.'

'Lesley,' Frances began tentatively, about to voice the dread which haunted her, 'you don't think he might be dead?'

'No, I don't. I think we'd feel it if he were.'

Frances recalled that Lesley was Scottish, and might also have the Sight, as Morag had done when she had prophesied a babe in her arms. How little she had thought then that her vision would come true! Lesley patted her shoulder awkwardly. 'You and I are going to be pals, us and the little one who is to be.'

This unexpected championship was too much for Frances in her overwrought state, and she began to weep.

'Hey, none of that!' Lesley protested. 'It's bad for the bairn. You've got to be strong, Fran, we've a lot to do.'

Frances sniffed and wiped her eyes.

'What?' she asked.

'As soon as we get to Glasgow you must visit a clinic, and I'll break the news to your in-laws. Then you'll have to meet them. They'll be glad because . . .' her own eyes filled and she turned away, 'if Gray never comes back, you've got all we have left of him.' She hastily overcame her weakness and went on: 'Then there's Crawfords, we've got to put some ginger into Sandy. He always was a pessimist.' She lifted her small chin defiantly. 'Crawfords must survive, for Gray's child.'

Frances was amazed. Lesley was four years younger than herself, but she had a drive and initiative that was lacking in both Ian and Sandy. Then she remembered that Gray had asked her to ensure that Alison and Sandy did not sell up. At the time she had taken little heed of his words, but it would almost seem he had foreseen this emergency. Haltingly she told Lesley about it, for the memory of that day on the Loch was hurtful. Lesley nodded.

'Yes, he believed in the business. Of course it's a

bad time, but I'm sure with energy and resource it can be made to pay.' Her face puckered. 'Silver Arrow carried a lot of prestige and I . . . loved that boat. I can't understand what happened, in fact there are a lot of things about this affair which don't add up, and I don't believe Stu Lambert has told all he knows. If only I could have gone instead of Sandy, I'm sure I could have dug something up. But Sandy will swallow any plausible tale, and Stu has the money . . . and the power . . . to do anything. Money talks.'

She sat down again on the bed, chin on hand, brooding. She looked like a young witch, weaving a spell. Frances watched her wonderingly. Not so long ago Lesley had tried to drown her, now she was offering her friendship and support. She did not doubt she could trust her. Lesley was a person of extremes, and having decided to transfer her loyalties, she would stand by her in any eventuality.

'You don't think Mr Lambert is telling the truth?' she asked.

'He may be as far as he knows it. I've nothing against old Stu, he's an honest man and he's fond of Gray, but he's got a son and a daughter who are not. Sam might do anything out of pique, if Gray rejects her, as he probably has, and Brett is a treacherous cad.'

She stood up and began to straighten Frances' bedclothes.

'You look fagged out, Fran—stay here and have a lie down, and I'll do the chores.'

This Frances knew was a noble gesture, for Lesley hated anything in the nature of housework, but she did feel exhausted and she lay thankfully down on the bed; she was more cheered than at any time since Gray's departure.

CHAPTER SEVEN

FRANCES sat in the swivel chair behind the opulent desk in the managerial office at Crawfords, which should of right been occupied by Gray. She was literally keeping his place warm for him. She was a privileged person now, for her grandfather had died, and as she was his only surviving relative, had left her a considerable sum of money. She could hardly be expected to grieve for someone whom she had never met and who had ostracised her parents, but she regretted that she had never attempted to contact him, for this benevolence suggested he had been lonely during his last years. The money was very welcome. She had invested the bulk of it in Crawfords and the much-needed capital had done much to set the firm upon its feet again. Her action, together with the birth of her son, had made her doubly acceptable to Gray's family. She had refused to call the boy Graham, saying there could be only one Gray, and had named him Robert, after his paternal grandfather, which was also the name of one of Scotland's most famous kings.

The office had caused friction with Sandy, who considered it was a waste of good accommodation to let it be unoccupied, but Frances had insisted it was

to be kept ready for Gray. She had it cleaned every
day, and fresh flowers placed on the desk in a slender silver vase which held one or two blooms. Often
she would sit in it herself when she came to call
at Crawfords, and go into a daydream, imagining
Gray walking in at the door, for both she and Lesley
were firm in their conviction that he was alive and
would one day return.

Most of his associates thought he must be dead, as
no trace of him had ever been discovered, in which
case Frances, as his widow, would inherit his large
holding of stock. Therefore she was humoured, amid
sorrowful headshaking. The puir lassie was deluded,
but as she was very sane upon every other subject, it
did no one any harm to let her have the office if it
comforted her.

Although she took no active part in the business,
she was keenly interested in all that appertained to
it. Today, Ian was showing her some designs for
canoes. Canoeing, he told her, was an increasingly
popular sport, and light, strong craft that were not
too expensive would find a market.

Both of them had changed. Ian had matured,
his features hardening into a more manly mould,
and he had gained in assurance, but though many
girls had tried to attract him, he never swerved in
his devotion to Frances.

She looked a little frail. She had not fully recovered from Robert's birth, which had been difficult, though the child was nearly six months old.
Her hair had been cut in hospital, and she wore it in
a shining bell to below her ears, and her face had
ripened into real beauty. In repose her mouth had a

wistful droop, and her eyes often had a faraway expression, but her manner was serene and gracious. She was dressed in a black woollen dress with white collar and cuffs, opening on to a V-shaped lace vest, and round her throat was a necklace of pearls, a present from her mother-in-law on Robbie's birth, which were no more silky than her skin. Lovely, aloof and unattainable, Ian thought as he watched her surreptitiously over his drawing board. Was she still grieving for the man who had treated her so cavalierly?

Frances and Lesley were sharing a flat with the baby, Murdoch and Caesar. Lesley was working in Crawfords' spare parts store, and often regretted the freedom of Craig Dhu. Mrs Crawford had gone to live with her daughter Alison, and Ian lodged with Margaret, with old Morag to look after them. They had sold their house, when Lesley announced that she was going to live with Frances, and had no room for Murdoch and Caesar. Frances had taken him in to care for the dog, and found he was an excellent baby-minder. He adored the wee bairn, as he called Robbie, and there seemed to be an affinity between the weatherbeaten Highlander and the small person who as yet could only express himself with coos and yells.

Ian pushed aside his board and looked at Frances intently.

'Are you going to wait all your life in the hope that Gray will come back?' he asked abruptly.

Frances turned her wedding ring absently on her finger.

'He's only been gone about fifteen months,' she

said slowly.

Her baby had done something to fill the gap, but she had never ceased to yearn for her husband.

'Only!' Ian exclaimed. He looked away from her towards the window which overlooked a drab street. 'In another nine months you could divorce him for desertion.'

Frances stared at him. 'Why on earth should I do that?'

'Because you're wasting your youth on a man who treated you badly,' Ian told her forcibly. 'He should either have taken you with him or let you alone. His only excuse is that he's probably dead . . .'

'No, he's not,' Frances interrupted. 'If he were I'd know it here.' She touched her breast, and Ian made an impatient movement.

'Very well then, but face it, Fran, he's left you, probably for another woman. He isn't worthy of your love and fidelity.' He leaned towards her, speaking low and earnestly. 'You should have a man to . . . to look after you. Robbie needs a father. I don't approve of one-parent families, they're incomplete.' He laid his hand over hers which lay on the desk, and his dark eyes sought hers, full of pleading. 'If you'd only marry me, Fran, I'd be so good to you. I wouldn't ask much of you, just the privilege of caring for you and your child. You must be often lonely, Les has her own life to lead, and will leave you in time. I've always loved you, right from the start, but of course with Gray around . . .' He made a grimace.

Frances looked down at his hand over hers, but

she made no attempt to withdraw it. She was touched by Ian's devotion, and she was lonely at times. Lesley was often out in the evenings, there was a young man at the works who was paying her attention, and though she derided the notion that there was anything between them, she did not seem to want to dismiss him. It was true what he said about Robbie, a boy needed a man. But Ian awoke no sexual response within her at all, never had done. Ironically he had all the other attributes to make a good husband, but the thing Gray had had in such abundance was lacking. She smiled sadly and said:

'Penelope waited twenty years for Ulysses to come back, but he returned in the end.'

'Yes, after having had a whale of time with Nausicaa, Circe and all the rest, while she, poor mutt, sat at her loom fending off her suitors. I don't think she was to be admired, I think she was a fool. You're a modern woman, Fran, you have rights poor Penelope never dreamed of. You shouldn't let yourself be neglected, sexually starved, abandoned. Besides, if Gray ever does come back, he'll be changed, and have formed other attachments . . .' Frances winced. What she feared was only too probable. 'Sorry, darling,' Ian noticed her expression, 'but do come out of your dreams and face realities. The life you're leading isn't normal.'

He stood up and came round the desk. Taking both her hands, he drew her to her feet. Holding them in his, he murmured softly:

'Oh, Fran, Fran, I love you so!'

The passion shining in his eyes momentarily stirred her, but only for a moment. He bowed his head and kissed first one hand and then the other, gently touching her fingertips with his lips. Frances looked down on his bowed dark head with a tender expression, wishing she could requite him, while she sought for the right words to soften her refusal. They made a pretty picture, the young man caressing her fingers, the woman with an almost maternal smile on her lips.

'What a charming scene! I'm afraid I'm intruding.'

The voice she had heard so many times in her dreams! Frances snatched her hands away and stared wildly at the door. It had been opened, and standing on the threshold was Gray. She rubbed her hand over her eyes, wondering if he were an hallucination, then stared again. He was still there. Incredulous with joy, she moved towards him, uttering an inarticulate cry, but the stony look he gave her caused her to halt. *Was* this Gray? He looked older and there were lines upon his face that had not been there before. His handsome mouth was set like an iron trap and his eyes as he surveyed her were colder than ice. He was immaculately dressed, in a perfectly tailored grey suit and waistcoat, blue shirt, and dark tie, but his sartorial elegance only emphasised his changed aspect.

Frances stood still, feeling her world was dissolving about her. So often she had envisaged this moment, when Gray did at last return to her. She had hoped for a tender greeting, a rapturous embrace, and then the revelation that she had borne him a son would surely move him. But the man regarding her so stonily was an inimical stranger. She glanced helplessly at Ian, who looked as bewildered as she did—worse, he looked guilty, though he had done nothing more than kiss her hands. But the intention had been there, he had been trying to steal Gray's wife, and he, with his uncanny perception, knew it.

Gray came up to the desk, and touched its shining surface. A muscle in his cheek twitched.

'My father's desk! Stu told me he was dying, but I . . . couldn't come.'

'He's dead now,' Ian said shortly.

'I know.' Gray turned a baleful eye upon the younger man. 'Have you usurped his place?' He looked contemptuously at the vase of flowers. 'And Fran has added the feminine touch. My father had no use for frivolities in business, nor women either.'

'Then he was all behind the times,' Ian declared, for Frances could not speak. 'Actually a woman has saved your business.'

Both were utterly dismayed by Gray's attitude. He seemed to be accusing them, but he was the one at fault.

Frances touched Ian's sleeve and shook her head. Now was not the moment to reveal what she had done for Crawfords. Gray marked the gesture.

'A conspiracy?' he asked, his voice dangerously soft.

Frances at last found her tongue.

'No, of course not. No one has usurped your place, Gray, I . . . we . . . kept this office in readiness for your return, hoping every day we would hear from you.'

'Couldn't you think of a more convincing lie than

that?' Gray sneered. 'I came straight here from the airport to find out what was going on. It seems I've been superseded, in more ways than one.' He pointed to Ian's drawing board. 'You've made yourself comfortable here.'

'That was . . . I only came in . . . Oh, but this is absurd, Gray. Arguing about an office when you've come back at last.' He moved eagerly towards the other man. 'Where have you been all this while? We feared you were dead.'

'You mean you hoped I was, but if you think I'm going to play Enoch Arden you're very much mistaken. I always thought he was a feeble character. I'm not going to steal away into the night, leaving you in possession. I'm the boss and you're all going to know it.'

'That's fine after being gone for over a year!' Ian was becoming angry, while Frances was dumbfounded. 'Of course we're delighted to see you, but . . .'

'Are you?' Gray's voice cracked like a whip, and Frances recalled with dismay that when he had come in Ian had been kissing her hands. He had always been jealous of her friendship with Ian and now he was putting the worst interpretation upon what he had seen. In the story of Enoch Arden, the husband had been away considerably longer than Gray had been, but the reference was clear. Enoch had gone away without revealing himself, but Gray had no intention of being so self-sacrificing, nor would she have wanted him to do so. She longed to throw herself into his arms, express her delight at his reappearance, but what was happening was a nightmare, and Ian was making things worse by being belligerent.

'We shan't be, if you talk like that,' said Ian. 'Really, Gray, you're the ruddy limit! You disappear, making yourself incommunicado, while your father dies and Fran grieves herself sick, to say nothing of your mother who needed you. Then you walk in and throw your weight about as if we were at fault. Aren't you going to give us some explanation?'

Very deliberately Gray walked behind the desk and seated himself in the swivel chair. Frances and Ian moved to either side of him and he looked from one to the other with a sardonic smile.

'I was detained in the States. There was something I had to do before I came back.'

'So you've been there all the time? But Lambert said he didn't know . . .'

'I forbade him to disclose my whereabouts.'

'Oh, did you?' Ian was smouldering with indignation on Frances' behalf. 'Was this . . . er . . . delay anything to do with Miss Samantha?'

'She was connected with it . . . yes.'

'Ah, now we're beginning to see daylight,' Ian declared triumphantly, while Frances moved to the window and leaned her head against the cool pane. The man who had come back was not the Gray who had gone away. He had become a hard, sneering stranger. Had Silver Arrow's mishap so embittered him that he was mentally affected? It was the kindest explanation, but Ian was trying to make him admit something more wounding, that he had lingered to dally with Samantha.

Ian said: 'Perhaps you've come back to arrange a divorce?' He was unable to keep the eagerness out of his eyes. Gray saw it and laughed.

'That would suit you, wouldn't it? But Fran won't want to marry a beggar, which is what you'll be when I've turned you out of Crawfords.' He looked at the slight black figure outlined against the window with a curious expression. 'I haven't finished with her yet.'

'She may have finished with you . . .'

Frances turned round from the window. 'Please, Ian,' she intervened gently. 'I want to talk to my husband alone.'

'Are you sure I'm still that?' Gray asked.

'I'm not sure about anything,' she returned steadily, 'except that you've changed. Please go, Ian.'

Reluctantly Ian left the room. Frances went round the desk and knelt beside Gray's chair. She took his unresponsive hand in both of hers and looked up appealingly into his face.

'I never believed you were dead,' she told him. 'But why didn't you send me some word? I've wanted you so, and the suspense was hard to bear. You've been very cruel, Gray.'

'I had my reasons,' he said harshly, 'and you're right, I have changed.' His hand gripped hers so hard it hurt, and looking down, she saw it was covered with white scars, his beautiful sensitive hand that had once caressed her so expertly.

'Oh, Gray, what have you done to it?'

He snatched it away and thrust it into his pocket. 'I burned it,' he said laconically. 'Get up, Fran, you know I hate sentimental scenes. The best thing you can do is as Ian suggests, divorce me.'

She stood up, feeling shattered.

'You want your freedom?' she asked dully.

'Don't you want yours?'

She thought of Robbie, but felt reluctant to tell this grim-faced stranger about the child.

'So Ian was right, it is Samantha,' she accused him.

He did not answer but picking up a pencil began to doodle on the clean blotting paper. He formed elaborate letters S, the initial of Samantha, and Silver Arrow. Reminded of the boat, she told him:

'Sandy was furious when he heard you'd sold Silver Arrow, he believes you squandered the money which he considers belonged to the company. I was surprised you had the heart to do it, but you wouldn't want to keep her when she'd let you down.'

As you don't want to keep me now you imagine I've played you false with Ian. But Frances did not say that.

He rose abruptly and walked to the window. Frances looked yearningly at his slim, graceful figure, which was as taut and lithe as it had ever been. Without looking at her, his eyes upon the street outside, he told her in a hard clipped tone:

'Silver Arrow was destroyed by a time-bomb— deliberate sabotage. The criminal was never discovered, but I knew, and Stu knew, it was Brett. Stu spent enormous sums to keep it out of the papers, and he sent Brett off on a world cruise to get him out of the way. He was horrified by what he'd done, but Brett was his only son.'

Frances stared at him aghast. She knew bombings and other violence were taking place every day, but they had always been remote. Lesley had hinted at sabotage, but no one had taken her seriously.

'Oh, Gray, how terrible! I'm so sorry.'

'Don't be a hypocrite,' he snapped. 'You always hated Silver Arrow.'

'But I know what she was to you. I meant it, I'm very sorry.' She recalled his scarred hand. 'Gray, were you there? Were you hurt?'

'I happened to come along at the wrong moment,' he smiled wryly. 'As a result I did have to go to hospital.'

Infinite reproach showed in Frances' eyes, and she took a step towards him. 'How could you keep us all in ignorance when such dreadful things were happening to you?' He shrugged and turned his head away. 'At least you might have let me know!'

He looked at her curiously. 'Why? What could you have done?'

'Come to you at once. I'm your wife, it was my place to be with you in your dark hour. I could perhaps have comforted you . . . a little . . .' Her lips trembled. 'Didn't you want me?'

A flicker of emotion showed in his eyes, to be instantly quenched, and he almost shouted at her:

'No! I didn't want you drooling inanities all over me. Besides, a woman's tongue can't be trusted. Stu paid for the best medical attention for me, and tried to pretend it couldn't have been Brett, but we both knew it was. I agreed that nobody in England should be told the truth, in case something leaked out. He was all for protecting that swine of a son of his, and I . . . I had my reasons.'

This repudiation and distrust hurt Frances almost unbearably. He had been injured and in distress, and had deliberately shut her out for what seemed to her to be very flimsy reasons. She said dully:

'I wonder you were able to conceal yourself, you're not exactly a nobody.'

'Everyone thought Graham Crawford had gone home with his tail between his legs. I was admitted to hospital as plain Mr Grey.'

The same name he had used on their honeymoon when he had made love to her so passionately. How little she meant to him that he could go through the worst experience of his life without even letting her know he was still alive. A body in a bed, that was all she had ever been to him, and there were other bodies equally accommodating. In a tight voice she enquired:

'Did Miss Lambert know where you were?'

'Sam? Oh, yes, she . . .' he hesitated, then went on, 'came to visit me.'

'So you didn't mind her coming?' Frances cried bitterly. '*She* was not excluded.'

'She was on the spot and in the know,' Gray explained. He smiled sardonically. 'She refused to be kept out.'

Frances felt a spurt of jealous anger.

'No, it was only me, your wife, you wanted kept out. Conveniently the Atlantic was between us and these fine friends of yours connived at keeping me in ignorance to suit their own ends. Yet I . . .' She checked herself. It was humiliating to speak of her love when he so obviously did not want it.

'I'd done my duty by you,' Gray told her coldly. 'If I died you were well provided for, as I promised when I asked you to marry me. Meanwhile you weren't in want, you were living with your friends the Fergusons, which was what you wanted to do, with Ian to comfort you. You refused to go to my people, which I thought was the better arrangement and more suitable. Now it's obvious why you wanted to remain with the Fergusons. I don't think you missed me.'

Not missed him, when with every fibre of her body, every thought in her mind she had yearned for him? Didn't he know she loved him? But he despised love and he felt none for her. He had had Samantha to 'drool' over him, as he put it, and shared his secret with her. She had been a congenial substitute for the deserted wife. Whatever injury Gray had sustained, he had made a complete recovery, except for his being thinner there was no physical change, but the loss of Silver Arrow had warped his mind, she could not get through to him, and he was using Ian as a barrier between them.

He did not know about Robbie, and how was he going to react to that news? Would it soften him? He looked as hard as his native granite. He might resent the child if he were wanting a divorce. No, she would not mention Robbie, not yet.

'You look quite fit now,' she began tentatively.

'I'm fine.'

'Then why have you waited so long to come back?'

'I had to wait for Brett's return.'

'Brett? But he . . .'

'I couldn't prosecute him, there wasn't enough evidence,' he said flatly. 'By the time I was discharged it was much too late to do anything officially, but I was going to get a confession out of him, and strike a blow for Silver Arrow. I had to wait some time to get him alone, and then . . .' his lips curled back in a smile that froze her blood. 'He was a white-livered hound, he admitted everything, and I had him begging for mercy before I'd done with him. I didn't quite kill him, for Stu's sake, but it'll be a long time before he drives a speedboat again.'

Silence fell between them. Frances sat down weakly on a high chair while Gray resumed his stare out of the window. Into that civilised room, with its polished furniture, silver vase of flowers, and leather-seated chairs, had crept a raw and primitive element that mocked its sophistication. Gray had taken the law into his own hands to avenge his wrongs. He had descended upon the unfortunate Brett like an avenging angel . . . or a devil. Deep within her Frances became aware of an involuntary response, that of ancestral woman to the fighting male, an atavistic urge towards her protector and mate, the guardian of the tribe, but it was not for her sake that Gray had meted out this savage punishment, but to avenge a craft that he had loved more than any woman.

At length Frances spoke.

'What do you propose to do now?'

Her words broke the ominous silence; the atmosphere became normal again. Gray turned from the window, the fixity of his expression relaxed to a tired indifference. He passed his hand wearily across his brow, the first indication of human weakness he had shown since he had come into the room.

'Oh, tidy up here, and after that, perhaps I'll go away again.'

'Back to Samantha?'

The words slipped out involuntarily, and he gave her a vindictive look.

'That would suit you, wouldn't it? So when two years are up you can divorce me for desertion. You may not find me quite so accommodating.'

'Oh, Gray!' Frances stood up and went towards him, her face full of desperate appeal. 'How can I convince you that there's nothing between me and Ian Ferguson, there never was and there never will be?'

'You can't. I have the evidence of my own eyes, they don't lie.'

Frances turned away with a half sob. She did not want to weep in his presence, but her throat was tight with tears. Their reunion should have been such a joyful occasion, but it had been ruined by Gray's premature entrance. A few moments later and she would have told Ian as gently as she could that his suit was hopeless, that her love was given to Gray for all time and she would never marry again. That was the Gray that was, not this embittered, biased stranger who scorned her love. Before her on the wall hung a framed photograph of Robert Crawford, the father-in-law she had never met. He had a kindlier face than his son's, but he lacked Gray's fine distinction, though he had the same arrogant lift of the head. He had left a widow who mourned him deeply. Better Gray had never come back then he should have returned so mistrustful and vengeful, then she could have retained the image of the gallant lover she had adored.

She became aware of a movement behind her, and Gray's hands, hard and punishing, gripped either side of her waist, and now there was a note in his voice she recognised as he said:

'You're still a desirable woman, Fran, and more beautiful than when I left you, and you're my wife.'

'So you've remembered that at last,' she retorted.

'I never forgot, though I think you had.'

Frances drew a quick breath, and put ineffectual fingers over his, trying to ease that merciless grip which she knew he meant to hurt. She turned her head, and their eyes met. For a fleeting instant she thought she glimpsed a desperate appeal in his, the torment of a suffering creature mutely begging to be released from the trap of its own pride and despair, but it was gone almost immediately, to be replaced by the cruel glint of metallic silver. He turned her about, shifting his hold, one hand in the small of her back, pressing her against him, the other at the nape of her neck, where her hair brushed his fingers.

'You've cut it off,' he remarked. 'Didn't Ian like it long? Or did the young man in Kent find he preferred you after all? I'd forgotten about him. To which will you run for consolation when I've finished with you? Because I'm going to claim my privileges before I free you.'

Frances closed her eyes to shut out the sight of the mocking devil lurking in his. What travesty of Gray had come back to her? But this was not the real

Gray, she told herself desperately; his body might be healed, but he was sick in his mind. Hoping to divert him, she said faintly:

'If you do that I can't divorce you for desertion.'

'Then we must find other grounds,' he told her silkily. 'How about . . . cruelty?'

He laughed with sadistic enjoyment as he felt her flinch. Wrapping both arms about her, he crushed her against him in a constricting embrace, using all his strength as if he would break her ribs. His mouth ravaged her face, throat, and neck with fierce demanding kisses, bruising her lips, grazing her skin. Frances struggled to free herself from this assault, but she was helpless against his muscles of steel. She wanted to reason with him, seek yet again to allay his unfounded suspicions, try to restore his sanity, but he was beyond the reach of words.

'Damn you, have you turned to ice?' he swore at her.

Deep within her, Frances felt passion stir in her body, but she would not respond to this savagery. Once Gray had wooed her with patience and gentleness to evoke the reciprocation he desired, now he was using violence and pain.

'Let me go, you brute!' she gasped.

He laughed derisively.

'You're my wife, Fran. I've a right to do with you what I will.'

He bent her backwards, his intention plain on his face, and her feet slipped on the polished floor as he bore her down.

'Gray,' she cried. 'For pity's sake! Someone may come in!'

The sound of running footsteps along the corridor outside indicated that someone was coming. Gray released her so suddenly she fell. He turned away, straightening his tie and pulling down his waistcoat. Frances scrambled to a chair, trying to adjust her collar to conceal the marks on her throat and neck, as Lesley burst into the room. Unaware of the tension in the air, she ran straight to Gray and threw her arms about his neck.

'Oh, Gray, Gray!' She was laughing and crying. 'You've come back!'

A spasm crossed the man's face, and for a moment he looked like his old self. He gently disengaged himself from Lesley's clinging arms and held her at arm's length.

'At least someone is glad to see me,' he remarked. 'But please don't weep over me, Les, you'll damp my shirt.'

'Damn your shirt,' she cried happily. 'Oh, this is marvellous!' She turned to Frances. 'Aren't you crazy with joy? Have you told him about Robbie?'

The mask had descended again and Gray's face and voice was full of suspicion as he demanded:

'Robbie? That's a new one. Who's Robbie?'

Frances was powerless to intervene. Not like this should Gray have been told about the birth of his son; but Lesley would suppose he had already been informed. She said now:

'Why, Fran's baby, of course . . .'

'Oh, Fran's had a baby, has she?' he cut in. 'Congratulations, Fran—you omitted to mention that little event. Were you so hot for Ian you couldn't wait to be sure I wasn't coming back?'

For a moment Frances did not grasp his meaning, then it hit her, and rage boiled up in her. She turned on him furiously, her eyes flashing.

'You cad, you brute!' she blazed. 'How dare you insinuate such beastly things! You leave me for your precious boat, get yourself involved in all sorts of thuggery, and haven't the decency to let me know you're still alive. I've done as you asked, tried to keep your business going, while you amused yourself with that American bitch. Then you come back to insult me, assault me, call me names. I hate you, loathe you, do you hear?'

Both Lesley and Gray were staring at her as if she had gone mad, it was so unlike the gentle Frances they knew to be so enraged. She rushed on, not caring:

'Robbie's mine, and I won't let you come near him, Gray, to contaminate him with your cynicism and base suggestions. God knows I loved you . . .' her voice broke, but she recovered and went on, 'but you scorned my love, and there are limits to what the greatest love can bear. You've killed mine. Go back to your Samantha and your American pals. I never want to see or speak to you again!'

She ran out of the office, slamming the door behind her.

CHAPTER EIGHT

FRANCES was in such a state of emotional turmoil that she had run out of the building and was half way down the street, before the cold wind recalled her to her surroundings and the realisation that she had left her coat and bag in Gray's office. She used public transport when she went to Crawfords, occasionally a taxi, for she did not own a car and had never learned to drive. She did not need one, living in a town. Her way lay through several not very salubrious streets before reaching the residential area where she lodged, and she preferred to avoid walking through them. The short afternoon was drawing to a close and the street lights had come on, as she stood biting her lip, wondering what to do. She shrank from returning to the building and running the risk of encountering Gray, and the only solution seemed to be to ring up Lesley and ask her to bring out her things. Would Lesley still be with Gray? She must risk that, and the chance that he might answer the telephone. Her present predicament would appeal to his saturnine humour, and he would tell her it served her right. She walked on looking for a telephone kiosk, and hoped that when she found one the instrument would be working. In these days of hooliganism there was no guarantee it would be.

Insufficiently clad, she was shivering, and when a car slid to a halt by the curb a little way ahead of her, she stared at it with lacklustre eyes. The driver got out and waylaid her.

'Mrs Crawford, are you all right?'

It was Lesley's boy-friend, Douglas Maxwell, and Frances stared at him blankly, trying to collect her wits. He was a well set up young fellow, with red hair, keen blue eyes and resolute chin. Though he and Lesley sparred, he never allowed her to ruffle him, and laughed at her more extravagant outbursts.

'Mrs Crawford,' he said more urgently, 'is something wrong? You look as though you've had a shock. Can I take you home?'

Frances recognised him with relief.

'That would be very kind of you, Doug. I . . . I've mislaid my handbag.'

Douglas firmly ushered her into the front seat of the car and wrapped a rug round her legs. He was not a man who wasted words and he thought Frances looked ill. As he started the car, he asked: 'Perhaps your bag was snatched? You've been attacked?' as that would account for her dishevelled appearance.

'I was,' she said dully, 'by a wild beast.'

She covered her face with her hands and shuddered, because that was how Gray had behaved, the man she had loved!

Douglas looked startled. Some ruffian must have accosted her, he thought.

'You ought to go to the police,' he said anxiously.

'They couldn't do anything.' Becoming aware of Douglas' anxious expression, she strove to speak more rationally. 'I can't tell you what happened, but it's not a police matter, nothing's been stolen. Lesley will bring my things. Just run me home, there's a dear, and I'll be all right.'

Douglas had a great admiration for Lesley's friend, and was a little in awe of her. She was quite an important person at Crawfords, besides being thought very beautiful and poised. To find her coatless on a winter afternoon walking the streets like a zombie was certainly surprising, but apparently nobody had been killed or injured and she obviously did not want to talk. So being tactful as well as kind, he asked no further questions, hoping Lesley would enlighten him, and drove her to her door.

'Shall I come up with you?'

'There's no need. Murdoch will be there. Thank you, Doug, ever so much. I don't know what I'd have done if you hadn't come along.'

'A pleasure, Mrs Crawford.'

He watched her go up the stairs to the next floor, still looking half dazed, and disappear through the door of her flat, wondering what could have happened at Crawfords to so upset her. That he never did learn, for Lesley was reticent, and no one in the firm ever knew the full story of the young master's return.

The door was not locked, so Frances was able to gain her bedroom without being seen. She changed her dress, bathed her face and neck, added some make-up and wound a chiffon scarf about her throat and felt somewhat restored.

The premises consisted of an upper storey flat, with two bedrooms, bath, kitchen and living room. There was an attic above where Murdoch and Caesar slept. The Highlander—his first name was Angus, though no one ever used it—was not only a domestic help, but he had proved an efficient baby-minder. Frances had no qualms about going out and leaving him in charge. He had acted as batman and cook to Gray, but a baby was something else.

He adored the 'wee maister', as he called Robbie, and a strange rapport existed between the old man and the infant.

Frances went into the sitting room where a bright fire burned and Robbie was strapped in his low chair, chewing a rusk. He was old enough to crawl now and Murdoch confined him to his chair when he was too busy to watch him all the time. The child was all Crawford, fair-haired, grey-eyed, and already he had Gray's imperious lift of the head. He was on the whole a good baby, sweet-tempered and contented, but he could when thwarted display a violent temper. He waved his rusk and crowed as Frances came in, and she bent down to kiss him. Caesar came to greet her, and sniffed at her skirt, then he whined and ran to the door. Frances knew that although she had changed, he had detected some lingering scent of Gray upon her.

'He's not there, old boy,' she said, scrambling to her feet, as Murdoch came in carrying a tray of tea for her. Sadly she went to sit by the fire. He should have been there, but he had not even asked where she was living.

Murdoch drew up a coffee table to her side and set his tray upon it.

'Ye be cauld, mistress,' he said, noticing her slight shiver as she thought of Gray. 'It be reet raw out.' He looked at Caesar. 'What's up wi' the dog?'

There was no point in prevaricating, he would have to know.

'Mr Graham's come back,' she said tonelessly.

'The good Lord be praised!' He looked eagerly at

the door. 'He be on his way?'

Frances shook her head. 'Mr Graham has formed other ties,' she told him in the same flat tone. 'Oh, he'll be seeing you before long, I'm sure, but we shan't be living together.'

Murdoch said nothing, though his face creased with disappointment. Robbie was demanding attention, and he lifted him out of his chair.

'I will bath the wean and put him to bed for ye,' he said kindly. 'Sit ye here and sup your tea, for I can see ye be chilled to the bone.'

Frances made no protest and smiled gratefully. She felt a great emptiness inside her. She had lived for months in anticipation of Gray's return; everything she had done had had that end in view. Now he had come, and her expectations had crumbled to dust.

She looked round the comfortable room which she and Lesley had furnished with part of her legacy. There was an open fireplace built of stone, plain beige walls with a few good reproductions of famous landscape artist pictures, a three-piece suite covered in bright cretonne; the tray on the coffee table was silver, the crockery bone china; they had been her grandfather's possessions. Caesar had gone back to the hearthrug, which his bulk obliterated. He twitched in his sleep; from the bathroom came the rumble of Murdoch's deep tones and Robbie's shouts of glee.

Gray's man, Gray's dog, and Gray's baby. He could claim the first two if he so desired, but she would fight tooth and nail to keep her child from him. Her sides were bruised from the grip of his hands, but that was nothing to the wounds to her susceptibilities. She no longer cared what had happened to him or what he was going to do so long as he left her and Robbie in peace. Lesley would have convinced him that Robbie was his child, nor did she believe he had really believed he was not. It had been another opportunity to insult her. Her mind reverted to Gray's story; it was an ugly one and he had cause for bitterness, but there was no excuse whatever for his long silence, except his perversity. A few words on a postcard could have relieved the worst of her anxiety.

She recalled the days in hospital when Robbie was born. The daytime had been bearable, the Fergusons and Mrs Crawford had visited her, but the evening hour, when the young husbands came from their work to see their wives and offspring, had been hard to bear. Gray had been in hospital too, but he had not wanted her, he had had Samantha to condole with him, to offer the sympathy he would not accept from her, the unwanted wife.

What would he do next? Appeal for restitution of conjugal rights? Was that the phrase solicitors used? Frances shivered, but not with cold. When she had told Murdoch they would not be living together, it was what she intended, but would Gray accept her decision, or would he force his way in here, disrupting her household, demanding his rights? She did not fear brutality, Gray's 'cruelty' would be much more subtle than that. He would exploit the physical attraction between them which her burning resentment could not entirely withstand for his own satisfaction, while he despised her for her acquiescence, and deny her his confidence and trust. That acid tongue of his would sear her tenderest feelings, and when he had tired of tormenting her he would go back to Samantha.

She could not endure it, she would not, but where could she find sanctuary? Lesley and his mother would support his claims. They would consider she should do her wifely duty, not understanding how deeply she had been wounded.

Murdoch called to her from the bedroom and she went in to say goodnight to Robbie. Rosy and sweet-smelling from his bath, he cuddled in her arms and sleepily nuzzled at her breast. He had been bottle-reared, as she had been unable to feed him herself, but he liked the comfort of the contact. As his long lashes closed over his eyes, she laid him down gently. This gift she owed to Gray, and she would always be grateful for it, but it was all she wanted now, and it was possible he might try to take the child from her. She did not reason that that would be difficult, for the mere thought threw her into a panic. She must go away, at once, before Gray sought her out and asserted his claims. When Lesley came in, much later than usual, she found Frances feverishly packing a suitcase.

'What on earth are you doing, Fran?'

'I'm going away,' Frances told her. 'You and Caesar can manage with Murdoch to look after you. I . . . I don't know how long I'll be gone, perhaps for good. I'll be staying at some small hotel while I look around.'

She thrust a packet of diapers into the case. Lesley sat down on a chair.

'If your flight has anything to do with Gray, it isn't necessary,' she said coolly. 'He asked me to give you a message from him, no doubt anticipating you might do something foolish. He'll respect your wish never to see him again. Were you afraid he'd force his way in here?'

This was an anti-climax to her fevered imaginings and, overcome, Frances sank down upon her bed.

'I . . . I thought it possible.'

'He's got more pride,' Lesley declared scornfully. 'Look, Fran, I don't know what happened between you, I don't want to know, but obviously it was not a tender reunion.'

'It was not,' Frances said emphatically.

Lesley sighed and shrugged her shoulders. 'You know your own business best. One thing more, since I seem to have been appointed go-between. What he told you about Silver Arrow and other matters is not to be broadcast, and he trusts you to hold your tongue. Officially Silver Arrow was sold, and Gray had important business in U.S.A. which kept him there.'

Through all her pain and bewilderment, Frances felt a faint gratification. He had told her the true story which he had not told to anyone else, and relied upon her to keep quiet about it. He could not believe her to be so utterly despicable after all. But he had not told her quite everything, not the part relating to Samantha, who was the 'business' that had delayed his return.

'I always thought there was more to the Silver Arrow saga,' Lesley went on, 'and I'm dying to know what happened, but of course I mustn't ask, if you're sworn to secrecy.'

'I am,' Frances said firmly, though she had made no promises. She would have liked to confide in Lesley, but without Gray's permission she would not utter a word.

Lesley stood up. 'I've brought your coat and bag. How on earth did you get back without money and in this east wind?'

'I met your boy-friend, Douglas,' Frances explained. She was glad to pass to a lighter subject. 'He gave me a lift.' She looked at her friend significantly. 'He's a nice lad, Les.'

'Not so bad.' The keen green eyes softened. 'We fight like cat and dog, but that keeps our association from becoming boring. Why he puts up with me, I can't imagine.'

'I think he loves you.'

Lesley laughed.

'Very perceptive of you, Fran. He hasn't said so yet, he's too canny to rush his fences, but if and when he does . . .' Her voice trailed away, and her lips curled in a little secret smile.

Frances smiled too; she was certain of the outcome. Poor Lesley had had her ups and downs, but she had got over her infatuation for Gray. Lesley looked at her hands.

'I must wash before supper, which I suppose the estimable Murdoch has prepared as usual. We shall miss him when he goes.'

'Why, does he want to leave?'

'Gray will want him back,' Lesley said over her shoulder as she moved towards the door. 'And he'll go running. Gray has a way of inspiring devotion in his underlings, or hadn't you noticed?'

She went to her own room, and Frances pushed the half-packed suitcase under the bed, with a feeling of chagrin. She had expected high drama, but Gray had retreated. His brief flare of passion had died away, leaving nothing but indifference. There was no need for her to run away, he had no intention of pursuing her. Contrarily she found this harder to bear than his threats. She had considered herself too important to him, and he was showing her that she meant nothing at all. His sojourn abroad had sundered them completely.

Over supper, Lesley told her what had happened at Crawfords after she had left. The place was in a furore and that was why she had been so late. The work force welcomed Gray with joy, he had always been popular with them, but the directors and semi-officials were glum. He had told them very definitely he was the man in command.

Information which rather contradicted his statement that he would be going away again, for why upset the applecart if he did not intend to stay? And if he did, where did Samantha fit into the picture?

'He won't really sack Ian, will he?' Frances asked anxiously.

'Did he say he would? If so Ian has forestalled him. He tendered his resignation immediately.'

'Oh, no!' Frances exclaimed, distressed.

'Oh yes. He says nothing would induce him to work under Gray after the way he's treated you, but that isn't all. Of course I told him what you'd done for Crawfords, and he insists you must be bought out.'

'Will that be possible?' Frances concealed her dismay, with difficulty, wondering what madness had got into Gray that he would cripple the firm sooner than accept her bounty.

'I don't know. Sandy is livid, especially as Gray hinted he might consent to a take-over by one of Stu Lambert's cronies. It seems poor Silver Arrow made quite an impression over there, in spite of the alleged defect. That Gray insists was not the fault of the workmen over here, he won't have them blamed.'

Frances, who knew they were not to blame, said drily:

'At least he's being fair to them.'

'Well, you see, his heart's not involved.'

'Heart!' Frances cried bitterly. 'Graham Crawford hasn't got a heart. All he ever felt for me was lust ... not a pretty word,' as Lesley looked shocked, 'but it's the truth.'

'Fran dear,' Lesley's green eyes surveyed her earnestly, 'Gray isn't himself. Those damned Lamberts have poisoned his mind. With patience and understanding he may come round, and only you can help him. You didn't mean it when you said you didn't want to see him again?'

'I did, and I'll stick to it,' Frances returned stormily. 'What he said and did,' she touched her side, 'was unpardonable. Why should I forever be his doormat? Accepting insults, desertion, probably infidelity with a smile?'

'Because you love him,' said Lesley.

Frances sprang to her feet.

'Not any more. Lesley, I'm through,' she cried

passionately.

'And Robbie?'

'Is my son, my child—Gray's part in him was only incidental.' She laughed angrily. 'I asked him once if he wanted children, do you know what he replied?'

Lesley shook her head.

'He'd like a son to be another speed ace.'

'But that was only natural,' Lesley said placatingly.

'Natural! To want to see his boy obsessed by one of those monsters, caring only for records and trophies, possibly being killed or maimed in pursuit of them.' Frances moved away from the table set before the fire. 'As if Silver Arrow hasn't caused me enough suffering without repeating the process!'

'Poor Silver Arrow,' Lesley mourned. 'She was a super boat.' She glanced at Frances' set face. 'But it's quite probable Robbie won't want to follow in Daddy's footsteps. He might prefer to collect butterflies.'

This suggestion was so incongruous Frances laughed with genuine merriment.

'Can you see Gray's son engaged in anything so frivolous? But you're right. Children don't always inherit parents' tastes, but Gray might try to persuade him.' She came back to the table. 'Has he asked to see him?'

Lesley shook her head. 'He's gone to see his mother. You can be sure Granny will sing his praises, she adores him. Gray will want to verify them.'

'I hope not,' sighed Frances. 'I think I shall go

away eventually. Back to Kent, I've still got acquaintances there and I'll have my dividends from Crawfords to live on until Robbie is old enough to go to school and I can take a job. That is if Gray doesn't run the firm into liquidation and if he buys me out I'll have the cash.'

'And leave me on my own?' Lesley asked reproachfully.

'My dear girl, before the year is out you'll be Mrs Douglas Maxwell!'

Lesley laughed and looked self-conscious. 'What a thought!' But she did not deny its possibility. 'But you can't deny Gray his son.'

'Much he cares about him!' Frances exclaimed. 'He might have surmised those . . . those nights at Rannoch Moor could have a result. But he never gave it a thought, he . . .'

She broke off. Unbidden, the inn had risen before her mental vision, the dormer windows and the stream; inside the low-beamed bedroom, Gray, her ardent lover, his bronzed body beside her on the bed, his head upon her breast. 'Oh, Gray!' she cried despairingly.

'You *do* love him still,' Lesley declared. 'You'll always love him, and it's said love conquers all things.'

'Sentimental twaddle,' Frances retorted. 'Gray taught me to despise romantic fallacies.' She looked at Lesley wistfully. 'He never loved me, you know.'

'I don't know,' Lesley said firmly. 'I think you're wrong there.'

'Well, if he ever did, he doesn't now,' Frances insisted.

'That's just it. If it had been anyone but you who he suspected of carrying on with Ian—I gather he caught you in a compromising situation—he'd just have laughed and told you to get on with it, but you were special, Fran.'

'So special he didn't bother to communicate with me for, how long is it? A year and three months.'

'Perhaps there were reasons . . .'

'There's only one that occurs to me, and that disproves your theories,' Frances returned. She moved restlessly. 'It's no good handing me soft soap—whatever was between us is finished. We're miles apart. I shall divorce him.'

The words had a finality that hurt, though she had declared their association was ended.

'It's what he wants,' she added defensively. 'And if I'm given custody of the child, he'll have no claim on him.'

Then she would feel safe—not that Gray showed any inclination to claim the boy, but Mrs Crawford might prevail upon him to change his mind, because she would not want to relinquish her grandson. Frances knew she would find the proceedings distasteful, but when they were over she could make her home in England, far from Scotland, Gray and all their painful associations.

'Divorce sounds so . . . so final,' Lesley protested. 'I suppose you can ask for alimony, or at least an allowance for Robbie's maintenance?'

'I don't want anything from Gray,' Frances declared passionately, 'only to be left alone in peace.'

Which was not quite true, but what she wanted he would never give her, never had; her only consolation was that she did not believe Gray had ever loved any woman.

As time passed, Murdoch became glummer and glummer. Frances knew it was because Gray had not contacted him. There was Caesar too, but Gray seemed to have forgotten about him. She had grown very fond of the great dog, he had been a comfort to her during the dark days of separation, offering her canine sympathy, as if he sensed her loneliness. He had attached himself to her, but he had not forgotten his master, as was proved by his excitement when he had detected his scent. When Craig Dhu was put up for sale, he had been a problem. Mrs Crawford did not like dogs, and the Fergusons' house was too small to accommodate him. The solution had been for Frances to have him when she had rented a place of her own, and Lesley had come to live with her, much to Margaret's displeasure. Frances did not think she could take him south with her, he was very large and expensive to keep, and he *was* Gray's dog. The old Gray would never abandon him, but the man who had come back from America seemed devoid of natural feelings.

Ian came to see Frances during the following week, rather to her dismay, for the accusations Gray had thrown at her made her feel guilty in his presence, innocent though she was. Gray had spoilt their friendship, as he had spoilt so much else.

Robbie was having his afternoon nap and she was alone when Murdoch showed him into the sitting room.

'I heard you hadn't been well,' he said, as if to excuse his visit. 'I came to see how you were.'

'I'm fine,' she assured him. 'Who told you I wasn't?'

'Doug.'

She had forgotten Douglas and Ian were friends, and she hoped the young man had not enlarged upon her appearance when he had picked her up.

'I was a little distraught,' she explained. 'Doug took me home the day . . . Gray came back.'

'And no wonder!' Ian became vociferous in his denunciations of his former employer. He had once thought the world of Gray and was all the more bitter because he had been disillusioned.

Frances expressed concern over his resignation, but he told her not to worry about that. There were plenty of openings for good draughtsmen, and he had been getting in a rut at Crawfords.

'But I never thought Gray could turn into such a louse,' he concluded.

'He's had a bad time.' Frances found herself wanting to defend her husband.

'Has he? He looks fit enough.' Ian was scornful, but he did not know what Frances knew. She recalled his scarred hands and wondered if Ian had noticed them. Apparently not.

'Lesley says you want to return to England,' Ian said.

'Eventually. I feel a clean break will be best for Robbie and me.'

'It's a shame!' Ian burst out. 'We were all so happy and contented until he came back. What a pity Silver Arrow didn't kill him before he sold her.'

'Oh, hush, Ian, you mustn't say that!' Frances was shocked. Nor had she been happy and contented with Gray's shadow ever at the back of her consciousness. Now the shadow had materialised into a grim reality, she hoped to be able to finally exorcise it. But to wish he had died, that she could never do.

'What's Gray doing?' she asked, suddenly hungry for news of him.

'Selling Crawfords to the Americans, apparently,' Ian told her dourly. 'He's living in a hotel—Sandy and he are at daggers drawn, so he could hardly go there. Mrs. Crawford is living with the McIntoshes, you know.'

'Yes, I did know.' So Gray had no home in Scotland, with Craig Dhu sold along with his father's house. That would not do anything to soften him. Suddenly her eyes filled with tears, all their efforts to put Crawfords on its feet had been wasted, and Gray was homeless in his own town.

'Not weeping for the bastard, are you?' Ian demanded.

Frances blinked. 'No, only for the sorry way things have turned out.'

'Poor Fran, you've had a rough deal. Remember, wherever you are and if you ever need help, you've one friend who will do anything for you if you call upon me.'

She thanked him, but she knew she would never turn to him. Once she had looked upon him as a sort of younger brother, but Gray had poisoned their friendship; his accusations would always be between them.

When he had gone, she watched him walk away through the sitting room window. He moved more purposefully than he had before. The change would do him good, all the same he too had had a rough deal. Why, oh, why couldn't she have fallen in love with him? As Gray had insisted she would? After a little initial opposition, they would have been happy, but now . . . She turned away from her contemplation of the empty street, with a deep sigh, as sounds from the bedroom indicated that Robbie had woken up. Whatever else had gone awry, she had her son.

CHAPTER NINE

IT was evening, some few days later. Robbie was in his cot asleep, while Lesley and Frances were sitting over the fire. It was unusual for Lesley to be at home, for her romance with Douglas was progressing, and she went out with him most nights, and Frances had to content herself with the company of Murdoch and Caesar. She made no complaint, because she was anxious for Douglas and Lesley to reach an understanding so that she would not feel she was deserting her friend when the time came to move south. She was thankful that the girl had recovered from her infatuation for Gray and had formed an attachment for another man. Lesley had not mentioned Gray since the day of his return and though Frances despised herself for wanting news of him, she often wished she would, but she was too proud to ask questions about him. He had taken her at her word and had made no attempt to contact her.

They heard the front door bell ring and looked at each other questioningly, for they rarely had visitors so late, and Frances felt her heartbeat quicken. Could it be Gray after all?

Murdoch threw open the door, and announced: 'Miss Lambert, mistress, to see you.' And Samantha came into the room.

Frances had only seen her the once, but her image was indelible. She was exactly the same as when she had come to Craig Dhu—round blue eyes, petulant expression, a mass of tinted hair, only then she had been in yachting garb, now she wore a mink coat over a trouser suit with a round fur cap on her head. She had long, high-heeled boots on her feet, beautifully cut and shaped to her legs, obviously handmade especially for her, and there were diamond studs in her ears. This was the girl who had caused Frances so much heartache, and she looked at her curiously, wondering what she had that she herself lacked. Money, that was obvious, but Frances could never bring herself to believe that Gray was mercenary.

Samantha looked round the room as if expecting to find another presence, but seeing only the two girls, she glanced from one to the other, drawing off fur gloves to show a plentitude of rings, including one on her engagement finger.

'Mrs Crawford?' she queried.

'I'm she,' said Frances. She rose from her seat. 'Do sit down. Shall I take your coat?'

Samantha clutched the fur about her. 'No, thank you—it's cold, even in here. Your central heating isn't very efficient.'

'We don't have it,' Lesley told her. She had not stood up, and was eyeing Samantha suspiciously.

'God, how ever do you survive?' She sank into Frances' chair and held out her hands to the blaze. Frances drew up a chair between them, aware that Samantha was scrutinising her closely.

'Why, you're the girl who was the home help at that impossible place further north,' she exclaimed. 'However did you manage to nobble Gray? I suppose you told him you were in the family way and the fool thought he ought to make you respectable.'

Frances flushed under the other girl's insolent stare, but her clouded eyes met the hard blue ones without flinching.

'It was nothing like that,' she said quietly.

Lesley was bristling in her chair.

'If you've only come to insult Fran, you'd better go,' she declared.

'Okay, no call to blow your top,' Samantha returned inelegantly. 'That's usually what happens to attractive maids when there are bachelors about, and married men too.' She giggled. 'And you are attractive, I give you that.' She was assessing Frances point by point. 'But these little romps don't last long. You've had your fun, and I've come to take Gray back where he belongs. I expected to find him here.'

'No, he is *not* here,' Lesley informed her. 'And we don't know where he's staying. You'd better enquire at Crawfords.'

Samantha looked pleased.

'Gee, that's just fine. So you are getting divorced?'

'I don't know what Graham's plans are,' said Frances stiffly, aware of a stab of pain at this finalising of her fears. 'Now you've found he isn't here, perhaps you'll go?'

How could he have involved himself with this doll of a woman? What possible chance of happiness had he with her? But Samantha had gone to him when he was incapacitated, insisted upon being admitted, when she, the wife, had been excluded. Perhaps her persistence had forged a bond between them, and he had welcomed her when his reluctance had been overcome. It was dreary enough in hospital without visitors, and possibly Samantha was more sympathetic than she looked. Frances was hating her for usurping her place. She should have been the one to solace Gray, but she had been deliberately kept in ignorance.

'I'll go when I've warmed up a bit,' Samantha announced. 'Gee, it's cold outside!' She gave Frances a reproachful look. 'I always understood you Scots were hospitable.'

'I'm not Scottish,' Frances told her, 'and you can hardly expect me to welcome you.'

'You're peeved because he prefers me to you?' Samantha asked. 'Well, I guess that's natural, though he's been away so long, you must have forgotten what he looks like.' Her words seemed to recall an unpleasant memory, because a look of disgust crossed her face. 'But he's quite recovered now, I saw him before he left.'

Lesley said: 'You're quite sure Gray will go back with you?'

'He'd better.' The hard eyes sparkled. 'He

assaulted my brother, a quite unprovoked attack, but Brett'll drop charges when Gray and I are offically engaged.'

'Unprovoked attack!' Frances exclaimed. 'When your brother had blown up his boat? Oh dear!' She looked guiltily at Lesley as she realised what she had said. Lesley looked satisfied; she had always believed something of the sort had happened to Silver Arrow, and was convinced Gray would never have sold her.

'That for a tale!' Samantha waved a diamond-bedecked hand. 'It was some terrorist gang, of course, they infiltrate everywhere, but poor Gray suffers from delusions since it occurred. When I get him back to the States, I'll take him to my head-shrinker, he's a good man and he'll straighten him out.' Her gaze sharpened. 'But how did you know about the explosion? I thought Pop had muzzled the press.'

'Gray told me,' Frances said simply.

'Oh, so you *have* seen him?'

Frances looked away. 'Just once.'

'That was most indiscreet,' Samantha declared. 'He shouldn't have contacted you at all. I thought he understood that when you said he'd not been here.' She frowned and looked into the fire. 'He insisted upon returning to Scotland to settle his affairs, though I tried to persuade him it wasn't necessary— he has relations here who could do that. Of course we plan to live in the States, that's why it's important he should placate Brett. He can't come back with charges hanging over his head. An apology should satisfy him since he's going to be Gray's brother-in-law.'

Lesley laughed outright.

'If you can see Gray apologising to that swine, it's you who needs your head examined,' she said scorn-fully.

Samantha ruffled like an angry hen.

'Really, Miss . . . er . . .'

'Ferguson. You were our guest at Craig Dhu, and I wish the lunch had poisoned you.'

'Gray shall make you take that back,' Samantha hissed. 'He won't stand for me being insulted!'

'Won't he?' said a voice from the doorway.

Caesar leaped up from the corner to which he had retreated when Samantha came in, and hurled himself upon the newcomer, whining with delight. Lesley cried, 'Oh, Gray, you've come at just the right moment!' but Frances stood motionless as if turned to stone. She had risen when Gray came in, and moved behind Samantha's chair, and his un-expected appearance had thrown her completely off balance. He had no doubt come to collect Murdoch and Caesar, but the sight of him had set her heart jerking. He looked more like his old self, some of the strain had left his face, and mouth and eyes looked more human. He was informally dressed, cord trous-ers and jacket over a Fair Isle pullover, which had something to do with it. Frances had so rarely seen him in a tailored suit at Craig Dhu. She wanted to appear cool and indifferent, but her quivering nerves warned her it would not be easy. However much her brain might condemn him, her traitorous body ached for him. But he ignored her completely, firstly being occupied with quietening the dog, and then rivetting his attention upon Samantha. The American girl stood up and went to meet him with outstretched hands.

'Hi, honey, didn't you get my wire? I thought you'd be at the airport to meet me, instead of which I've been chasing all round this burgh trying to locate you.'

Gray put his hands behind his back.

'You didn't send a wire, Sam, nor any other message, and how the hell did you get hold of this address?'

Samantha giggled. 'It was in the telephone directory, sweetie, Mrs F. Crawford, and I thought that she . . .' she jerked her head towards Frances, 'would know your whereabouts.'

'I don't want you here,' Gray told her shortly.

'What's the harm? Lots of women are good friends with their husbands' exes. It's the civilised way to behave.'

'Fran is not my ex,' he returned.

'But she soon will be,' Samantha persisted. 'Darling, you don't seem pleased to see me at all, and I've come all this way to warn you Brett's threatening proceedings against you for assault.'

'He'll be a fool if he tries to prosecute me,' Gray told her grimly. 'Does he want the whole affair dragged out into the open after the pots of money your father paid out to keep it quiet? I shan't hold my tongue in court.'

'But you've no proof it was Brett,' Samantha protested, forgetting her previous statement that he was not the culprit.

'He had a motive which no one else had, and I don't think your family want the ugly story made public.'

Samantha shrugged her shoulders.

'Such a fuss about an old boat! Oh, I know you got injured, but Brett never meant to harm you. How was he to know you'd be prowling round the marina when you should have been in bed? The wonder is the security guards didn't arrest you.'

'They'd already been bribed to pass Brett through, and I could hardly be denied access to my own boat.' Gray glanced at Lesley and frowned. 'Of course you would have to blab. None of this was known over here, unless Fran talked.'

'She didn't,' Lesley broke in. 'She's much too loyal to betray your murky secrets, but I never believed you'd sold Silver Arrow. Go on, this is interesting. How badly were you hurt?'

'Oh, he's fine now,' Samantha intervened. She went closer to Gray and took hold of the lapels of his jacket, gazing ardently into his unresponsive face.

'Darling, that's all over and done with. Come back with me now, and we'll square Brett. He won't prosecute one of the family.'

'I'd see you in hell before I'd unite myself with your family,' Gray said so softly his meaning was not immediately plain. He disengaged her clinging fingers. 'I told you when I said goodbye to your father, I was going back to my wife.'

Samantha scowled at Frances, who was still standing like a pale effigy in the background. Gray seemed to be repudiating Samantha, but then he had also repudiated her, when he had tired of her.

'That whey-faced ninny!' Sam spat out the words like an angry cat. 'What can she give you except a parcel of brats? Pop could build you another Silver

Arrow.'

'I don't want one. All that's finished.'

'Is that so? But don't you owe us something, gratitude at least, for all your fees at that expensive sanatorium, where you had the most modern medical
attention? You look much as you always did, but
when I came to see you I thought you were disfigured for life.'

'Yes, you came once.' Gray's face was like stone.
'And you ran out shrieking like a startled peacock
when you saw what your delightful brother had
done to me. You never came near me again.'

Frances drew a long breath at this revelation. She
was beginning to perceive that as far as Samantha
was concerned she had been completely in error.
Far from being a ministering angel, Samantha had
fled from the sight of . . . what? Burns? Scars? She
glanced at his hands . . . like that? But his face was
as smooth and unmarked as it had always been. Was
one of them lying?

Samantha shrugged her shoulders petulantly.

'You didn't realise now terribly sensitive I am. I
hadn't been warned, and your appearance gave me
an awful shock,' she defended herself. 'I didn't come
again because I was sure you wouldn't *want* anyone to
see you looking like that.'

Gray glanced at Frances, who had turned very
white.

'Quite so,' he said drily. 'But if you had a shock,
you'd only yourself to blame. You pushed yourself in
uninvited when I'd implicitly stated I would not see
anybody.'

He turned his back on Samantha and stooped to

caress his dog. Frances felt stunned as she absorbed the real reason for his long silence. He must have been far more badly hurt than he had led them to suppose. It was not Samantha who had kept him from her, but ... what? Vanity? Gray had never seemed the least conscious of his looks. Pride? His masculine arrogance shrank from allowing her to see him weak and suffering, that and lack of trust; he must have believed she would have been revolted by a scarred face.

Lesley said: 'But you look your handsome self, Gray.'

He returned laconically: 'Skin grafting.'

Frances did not know much about that except that it was a long and painful process, but she was deeply wounded to learn that Gray had gone through so much without asking for her or even permitting her to be informed of what had happened to him. His lack of faith hurt more than his caustic words when he had found her with Ian and dried up the flood of pity that had welled up in her at Samantha's revelation. With regard to Ian, he had some excuse, he had seen him kissing her hands, but to deliberately keep her in ignorance of the ordeal he had come through showed a distrust that filled her with anguish. She would not have turned from him if he had been disfigured for life, he was her husband, whom she loved, but he classed her with the heartless nitwit he had just repulsed. She said to the back of his head, as he bent over the dog:

'Oh, Gray, you might have died!'

'I nearly did. Pity, wasn't it, that I survived? It would have been so convenient for all concerned if

I'd kicked the bucket.'

'Oh, don't say that!' Samantha wailed. 'My heart would have been broken.'

'You haven't got one.' He stood up and looked her up and down scathingly. 'You only wanted me when I was on top of the world. When you thought I might be crippled you fled. I suppose you've come after me because you imagine I'll again be a glamorous racing pilot, but it's no go, Sam. All that's over. Graham Crawford, speed ace, died when Silver Arrow was destroyed. I'm grateful for all your father did for me, but I think he owed it to me. As for you and your louse of a brother, I've no use for you whatever. Nor would I ever want to live in your country. Scotland's my home and here I shall bide. Now get out!'

Samantha drew herself up like a snake about to strike. All trace of prettiness had vanished, she was all teeth, staring eyes and spitting venom.

'I'll make you pay for this, Gray Crawford, you see if I don't!'

'I think,' he said more gently, 'I have already paid.'

Caesar, sensing the menace in Samantha, gave a growl, and Gray put his hand on the dog's collar.

'My sentiments exactly,' he smiled wryly. 'Come off it, Sam, there's better fish in the sea waiting to be hooked. You'll soon forget me.'

'That I can't,' she retorted, the fury dying out of her face. She looked almost sad. 'You may be a swine, Gray Crawford, and you've only contempt for women, but no girl who has loved you could ever forget you.'

With which parting shot, she flounced out of the room.

'Unfortunately Sam Lambert doesn't know what love is,' Gray said to no one in particular.

'No more do you,' Frances told him bitterly, for in his darkest hour he had not turned to her but had shut her out.

'Of course you're the expert,' he returned sarcastically. 'Sorry about that scene—I'd no idea she'd follow me here. Some women can't take no for an answer.'

'Since you are here, do sit down and let me get you a drink,' Lesley invited him. 'I'm glad she came, because now I'm in the picture. So dear Brett put a time-bomb in your boat so she couldn't compete, and got you too by mistake. Quite enough to drive you round the bend, but I'd like to hear more about your time in hospital.'

'I daresay you would,' he returned coolly, 'but I've no intention of satisfying your curiosity. That too is finished.' He turned to Frances apologetically. 'Forgive me for intruding upon you, and I won't stay, because I know you don't want to see me. I called expecting to see only Murdoch, as I intended to take Caesar for a walk.' His face softened as he stroked the dog's head. 'My faithful hound,' he murmured. 'You don't change.' He looked at Frances again and his eyes were ice. 'When Murdoch said Sam was here I thought I'd better come in and put the record straight.'

'I'm glad you did,' Frances said equally coldly. 'But how did you know the dog was here?'

'My mother told me, and also that Ian Ferguson

was a frequent visitor.' Lesley uttered an exalama-
tion and Frances thought despairingly how gossip
could distort the most innocent happening. Ian had
called once and must have been seen by some busy-
body who had exaggerated. Gray went on:

'I suppose he comes expecting you to condole
with him about leaving Crawfords, but I didn't fire
him, he fired himself.'

'So he told me,' said Frances, and could have
bitten her tongue out, for that admission would
seem to confirm that he called often. Gray gave her
a veiled look, and told her:

'I'm very grateful to you for taking care of
Caesar. I should have been very distressed if he'd
been destroyed.'

'I couldn't let that happen,' Frances assured him
quickly. 'I love him too.' She hesitated. 'Will you
bring him back?'

'If I may. Otherwise, as I'm living in a hotel, it
would have to be kennels, which he'd hate.'

'He's more than welcome here.'

'More than I am.' Gray's smile was twisted.

'Oh, Gray!' Frances with difficulty restrained a
rush of tears. Gray's concern for his dog had
touched her in spite of herself, but he had to go and
spoil it with an unfair dig at her.

'Why do you say everything you can to make me
hate you?' she asked despairingly.

'Do I?' He looked mildly interested. 'It isn't in-
tentional.'

He hesitated as if considering what to say next,
and Lesley broke in eagerly:

'Gray, since you're here . . .'

He interrupted her quickly as if he knew what she was about to say.

'I mustn't stay. It's getting late and it'll be very late when I bring Caesar back. I'm sure Murdoch won't mind waiting up to let the hound in, so I need not disturb you.' He smiled, his old charming smile, as he looked at Frances, and her heart seemed to melt. 'I see you took pity on him too, Fran. The poor old chap nearly wept on my shoulder when he opened the door to me.' He paused, seemed to consider, and Lesley looked at him appealingly, while Frances' eyes were wistful, but all he said was:

'Have you got Caesar's lead?'

'It's hanging up in the lobby.' Frances moved towards the door, anxious to conceal her emotion. For a moment Gray had looked so like he used to do that she had to restrain an impulse to throw herself into his arms. That such a thought was far from his mind was only too obvious.

'Don't bother, I'll find it.' He opened the door, but turned back again, his hand on the knob. 'I'll be making some financial arrangement for you, Fran, but Sandy will act as my intermediary, so you won't be troubled by my obnoxious presence. Goodnight, ladies.'

He went out followed by Caesar, closing the door behind him.

Lesley exclaimed indignantly:

'He isn't human! All that concern for Caesar and he never asked about Robbie, let alone wanted to see him. Isn't a child more important than a dog?'

'The dog's his, and he still isn't sure about Robbie!' Frances said bitterly.

'You can be certain his mother's put him right about that,' Lesley declared emphatically. 'You've only to look at the bairn . . .'

'Which Gray very obviously doesn't want to do.'

Before Samantha's coming, she would have ascribed his reluctance to his desire for a divorce. Robbie could only complicate proceedings, but she had been quite wrong about that. Yet she felt no elation at Sam's discomfiture. The barrier between her and her husband seemed to remain impenetrable. Ian still stood between them. She sighed.

'Someone's reported that Ian came to see me . . . with embellishments.'

'So what? You're not in purdah.' Lesley sat down again by the fire and seemed to be ruminating. 'I'm glad to know the truth about Silver Arrow at last,' she said, 'but Gray's attitude is inexplicable.' She looked at Frances half shyly. 'He puts me in mind of the fairy story about the Snow Queen . . . you read it as a child, of course?' Frances nodded. 'Splinters from the goblin's evil mirror entered Kay's heart and eye. The former became devoid of feeling, the vision of the latter was distorted, so all that was fair seemed foul. One could imagine that fragments from the bomb which destroyed Silver Arrow had the same effect upon Gray.'

'A bit far-fetched.' Frances was surprised that the practical Lesley should harbour such a whimsical notion.

Lesley looked at her meaningly. 'Kay was restored by the devotion of little Gerda. It was her tears which melted the splinter in Kay's heart and caused the other to fall from his eye. I believe that if you tried . . .'

Frances had suspected whither Lesley's fantasy was leading, and her face hardened.

'No, I'm not going to crawl to him and be spurned,' she said firmly. 'I've taken as much as I can stand from him.'

Desire had flared up in him during that painful scene in the office, but now even that seemed to have died.

'Since you've fallen in love yourself you want every story to have a happy ending,' she went on, lifting her head defiantly. 'Mine will too, because I've got Robbie and I'll make a new life with him. I'm relieved Gray isn't interested in him, it means no one will dispute my sole claim to him.'

'But as Sam said, no girl who has loved Gray can ever forget him,' Lesley protested. 'I'll always have a special feeling for him myself, though I was never in the running.'

'Oh, I shan't forget him entirely,' Frances strove to speak lightly. 'He made too deep an impression for that to be possible.' In spite of her brave front her eyes filled with tears and she looked away hastily, hoping Lesley had not noticed. Craig Dhu, the lochan in the hills, the rhododendrons and the waterlilies, and the white sands of Morar, were all enshrined in her heart, memories to be recalled during the years ahead when they had lost their pain but never their poignancy.

'You'd better go to bed,' she resumed. 'Murdoch will wait up for Caesar and you have to be up in good time to go to work.'

Lesley stood up, smoothing down her skirt.

'Doug doesn't want me to go on working after we're married,' she announced, 'and I shan't be sorry to give up. Dealing out spares and invoicing stock isn't like the fun it was at Craig Dhu, servicing Silver Arrow and the other boats. I'm nothing more than a clerk nowadays.'

Both became silent, seeing in retrospect the sunlit loch and the passage of the arrow-swift speedboat, and its owner, lighthearted and debonair, so confident of its success.

Lesley gave a long sigh.

'You coming? Not going to sit brooding here?'

'No. I'll be coming when I've spoken to Murdoch. Goodnight, Les.'

Lesley put her arm round her friend's shoulder and kissed her, which was a rare occurrence with her, as she was not demonstrative.

'We've come a long way since I pushed you into the loch,' she said with a wry smile. 'I've learned to appreciate you, Fran, if Gray hasn't. I'll tell you something—Doug's all right, but if he went off into the blue for over a year, he wouldn't find me waiting for him. But the saints of this world are never recognised until after they're dead. Goodnight, Fran.'

CHAPTER TEN

FRANCES went into her own room and roused the sleeping Robbie to change him. He made no demur about this necessary proceeding, sinking back into sleep as soon as she returned him to his cot, contentedly sucking his thumb.

Frances sat down upon her bed and involuntarily her thoughts turned to Gray. Picture after picture filtered through her mind—Gray putting on her sandals at Morar, recalling her to life after she had been half drowned in the loch, teaching her to swim, the sunlight on his hair and his splendid bronzed body, Gray proposing to her in the boat, suggesting a marriage of convenience, that was, however, to be consummated. The nights at the inn, Gray dancing the sword dance, and his departure in the misty grey morning exhilarated by the prospect of success.

'I'll crown you with my laurels.'

Always he had been a dominant vital figure, bending her to his will. Samantha's visit had been a revelation, dimly she began to perceive why he had not wanted her to come to him. His masculine pride could not bear that she should see him defeated and disfigured, he who had been to her like a pagan god, Jupiter falling upon Danae in a shower of gold, Apollo the invincible. She would not have shrunk from him whatever he had looked like, but he would have hated to see pity in her eyes. Only if he had truly loved her could he have accepted her sympathy, turned to her for solace, but he had never loved her, never perjured himself to the extent of saying that he did, as many men would in the throes of desire, nor had he asked her for love, demanding only reciprocation and loyalty. If they had not been parted, he might have come to love her as well as desiring her body, and that had been her great hope, but fate decreed otherwise.

He *had* been coming back to her, and unluckily had surprised her with Ian. Already embittered by his experiences, distrustful of his so-called friends, he had immediately jumped to the wrong conclusion. Their courtship and marriage had been so brief he could all too easily believe that she had found consolation with a man for whom he had always suspected she had a softness. As for his assault upon her, that had been prompted by an urge to reassert his mastery over her, a bitter revenge for her apparent infidelity. Now he appeared to have accepted the situation as he imagined it to be. Her outburst when she had declared that she never wanted to see him again had convinced him that she would never forgive the outrage he had sought to inflict upon her.

Lesley was right—she did still love him, always would, however cruelly and indifferently he treated her. There was something about him that made it impossible for a woman to forget him. And there was Robbie. Gray would know now that the child must be his, but he had not asked about him or wanted to see him. Perhaps he felt that it was better to ignore him if they were going to part. Part? Her heart contracted. Could she bear to be legally parted from Gray, slight though her hold upon him was?

She had told Lesley that she would not crawl to him, but it was the woman's role to be generous and forgiving, and she was the one who loved. Would it not be worth while to make a further effort to arrive at a better understanding, now she knew that Samantha did not stand between them?

He would be bringing the dog back, expecting Murdoch to let him in. She wondered where they had gone. Probably he had driven out to some open space where Caesar could run. She went to look out of the window. It was a fine starry night, though cold, and white hoar-frost lay over the roofs. That would not deter them, but both would be chilled by the time they returned. Frances came to a decision. She would send Murdoch to bed, and open the door to them herself, invite Gray to come in and offer him a chance to warm himself and some refreshment.

Excited by the prospect, she went into the sitting room and made up the fire. From a cupboard she took out glasses and the whisky they kept for chance visitors. Then she went to find Murdoch, who was sitting over the stove in the kitchen.

The old man looked at her eagerly.

'The maister will be staying the neet?'

She shook her head. 'He's staying at a hotel until I . . . we . . . there's not much room here, is there?'

The shrewd eyes surveyed her. She did not look like a happy wife, rejoicing in her man's reappearance; she was very pale, and her big eyes were wistful.

'The Crawfords are a proud race,' he told her. 'But Mister Graham is a fine mon, for all he left you grieving this long while. What they've done to him over yon has hurt him sair, but he'll no own to it. Ye're a brave lassie, mistress, and I reckon only you can reach him. His mither . . .' he shrugged his shoulders, 'they were never close, and the auld mon's gone, who thought the world of him. He's nobbut you to turn to, to make him whole.'

'I'll do what I can,' Frances promised, praying he was right. 'Go to bed, Murdoch, and I'll wait up to let him in.'

The old man chuckled. 'He sent that foreign bitch awa' with a flea in her ear, that's one good riddance! Be gentle with him, mistress, and God be wi' ye.'

He left to go up to his attic room, and Frances went to hers. She changed into the black lace dress she had worn on her wedding night, and carefully made up her face. She looked at her watch. They could not be much longer, for Gray would not keep Murdoch up all night and it was nearly midnight.

She went back into the sitting room and turned the stereo on, thinking a little soft music might help. An orchestra was playing the Peer Gynt Suite, and the hunting strains of Solveig's Song stole out into the room.

'The winter may pass and the spring may die . . .
. . . but thou wilt come again, and I will await thee . . .'

Impatiently Frances switched it off. Penelope, Annie Arden, Solveig . . . all women who waited patiently for their men to return to them with unquestioning love, and all created by men, idealising feminine patience and fidelity. Had they any connection with modern life where such virtues were more pitied than praised? Throughout the ages women had always waited while their menfolk went forth to do and dare, but Women's Lib was seeking to change all that. Frances smiled wryly. Gray would scorn the aims of Women's Lib, but he would not take them seriously, he was so superbly masculine he assumed superiority as of right.

She could not sit still, but wandered restlessly about the room, every nerve taut, fearful that Gray would spurn her overture. She prayed that she might find the right words to reach him.

At last her straining ears caught the sound of the outer door handle being turned. As he found the door locked there followed a discreet tap; he would not risk disturbing them by ringing the bell. Caesar whined plaintively.

Frances ran to open it, and the dog pushed past her.

'Gray!' she called.

He was already moving away, but at the sound of her voice, he turned back.

'Fran! You shouldn't have stayed up. I told Murdoch . . .'

'I sent him to bed. I . . . I must talk to you, Gray.'

'Indeed? What a change of front!'

The light from the open door spilled over him, but did not reach his face. His voice held the mocking timbre she loathed.

'Oh, do come in, it's freezing with the door open,' she cried impatiently, and as he did not move, she added anxiously: 'I promise I won't keep you long.'

He hesitated, and she waited in trepidation. If he refused her now, she would know it was hopeless. The glimpse of the bright fire through the open sitting room door seemed to decide him. Caesar was already stretched in front of it. To her relief he stepped inside and she closed the door and locked it.

'Let me take your coat.'

In silence he slipped off the suede coat he had put on for his walk, and Frances hung it on a peg in the lobby. The intimacy of the gesture heartened her. She was very conscious of his presence close behind her. He followed her into the sitting room, and sat down in the chair she indicated, holding his hands to the blaze. His face was inscrutable.

'A drink?' Frances suggested briskly.

He turned his head to look at her, his eyes travelling over her black-clad figure, and she wondered if he recognised the dress; it must be obvious to him that she had changed since Samantha left. His glance went to the whisky bottle.

'Thank you, if you'll join me.'

She poured a generous measure for him, and one mostly soda water for herself, moving the coffee table towards him to accommodate his glass. He looked up at her with a sardonic glint in his eyes.

'What's all this? The fatted calf for the prodigal's return? Isn't it a little late in the day?'

She ignored the crack, and seated herself opposite to him on the other side of the fireplace. Caesar, finding the fire too hot, got up and removed himself to a far corner. Frances took a sip of her drink, wondering how to begin. He had a preoccupied air as if he were thinking of something else, which did not help. She noticed there were silver threads among the fair hair on his temples, though he was not much more than thirty. Her eyes fell on his hands held out to the fire, marred with the ridges of white scar.

'Was your face as badly burned as your hands?' she asked.

He nodded. 'They wanted to treat my hands too, but I could wait no longer. The process takes such a long time, they can only do a little at a time, and the damage was fairly extensive.'

He gave the information in a quiet, matter-of-fact tone, his eyes on the glowing coals. Forgetting she had meant not to reproach him, Frances cried:

'Oh, Gray, you should have let me know. I'd have come to you, I wouldn't have let anything stop me.'

'As I told you, that's what I wanted to avoid.'

'But it wasn't fair! I'm your wife, it was my privilege to comfort you.'

He moved restlessly, and said coldly:

'Do you think I wanted you to see me as an object of pity? Poor disfigured Gray! No, my girl, you had to wait until I was presentable again.'

'As if it would have made any difference to me what you looked like!'

'Wouldn't it?' He held out his hand. 'That shows you how I would have appeared without the treatment, and the doctors weren't sure it would be wholly successful.'

Frances gave a low, inarticulate murmur and dropped on her knees beside him, raising his scarred hand to her lips. Gray smiled sardonically down upon her bent black head.

'A pretty gesture, Fran, but that's only my hand.' He gently withdrew it from her clasp and reached for the whisky. Frances sat back on her heels regarding him with misty, reproachful eyes.

'Altogether I was a loathsome-looking object, with bandages, plastic and whatnot.' He took a gulp of his drink. 'Sam's reaction was not encouraging.'

Samantha who had run screeching from the hospital.

'I'm not Sam,' Frances said indignantly.

'You certainly aren't, and you'd have put up a fine façade, I don't doubt, but you wouldn't have been able to deceive me.'

'You could at least have let me know you were alive.'

'No one could be sure how successful the operations would be. I wanted you to remember me as I was, and if I were going to be scarred for life, I wouldn't have come back at all.'

'You'd no faith in my love?'

He smiled. 'Did you love me, Fran? I don't see how you could. I bulldozed into your life, married you in haste and then deserted you. Of course, we had a charming idyll, but you're young and romantic, I didn't think you'd appreciate your Prince Charming turning into a gargoyle.'

Frances sighed. How dense he was! But then he never had taken love seriously, he did not believe it went more than skin deep. Skin ... She looked at his hands; they had not been treated, but she did not shrink from them.

'The truth is you didn't want me ...' she began sadly.

He turned towards her, with a sudden blaze in his eyes.

'Want you?' he cut in. 'I wanted you every hour I

was in that damned place! I longed for a sight of you, but if you'd been revolted as Sam was, I think I'd have killed myself!'

He had erupted into sudden life, and his voice shook with passion, then his emotion died as quickly as it had come. He drained his glass, and went on quietly, his gaze returning to the fire. 'I lost all sense of time while those sadists were working on me. Stu told me about my father's death, but I was in no fit state to travel when it occurred. I heard Sandy came to fetch me, and Stu put him off. He's been a very good friend.' He passed his hand over his eyes. 'I . . . I was sorry about my old man, I . . . cared for him.' He was silent for a moment, and Frances realised it was the first time she had heard him express affection for anyone. He went on:

'While I was waiting for my face to heal, I regained my bodily strength. I needed that, because before I left I was going to settle my score with Brett. I owed Silver Arrow that.'

Frances had remained on the floor at his feet throughout this recital. She had thrilled when Gray had said he had longed for her, there was hope yet, but she deplored the fierce pride which had kept him from sending for her. She could have done so much to alleviate his convalescence. He had denied himself what she would have been only too willing to give. Then she remembered that while he had been languishing in a sanatorium, she had been thickening with his child. How would he have reacted to the sight of her ungainly figure? Would he in his turn have been revolted? Was the outward seeming so important that a physical change could kill love? In her own case she was confident that it could not, but Gray had never loved her, he had only desired her for her looks, and if they had been spoiled, would he have welcomed her? He had said he had longed for the sight of her, but it was the girl of the white sands and the swimming pool he had envisaged, not a matron nearing her time.

She said wistfully: 'It might have made a difference if you'd ever been in love with me.'

He turned his head and stared at her blankly.

'Good lord, woman, what are you talking about? I was as much in love with you as a man can be with a woman. You were all I wanted, beautiful, passionate, reliable, loyal . . . or so I thought. Why else did you think I married you?'

'That wasn't among the reasons you gave me when you asked me,' she pointed out, noticing with an uneasy qualm that he had used the past tense.

He smiled ruefully.

'Well, it was difficult . . . you were so aloof and virginal, Fran, I daren't tell you I was burning to possess you before I went away, you'd have been shocked. So I thought up other and more respectable reasons, and they were quite genuine. I hated seeing you waiting upon the Fergusons, and I wanted to give you security, but you refused to go to my parents, which was what I intended, and instead of being proud to be my wife, you wanted our marriage kept a secret. Later on when I had time—oh, much too much time—to review your motives I decided you wanted to return to Craig Dhu to keep tabs on Ian. He was your second string if I didn't come back.'

'Oh, Gray . . .' she tried to interrupt, but he went on regardless.

'I didn't blame you. A woman in your position had to look to the future, and marriage was your best bid. You knew me so little you'd no reason to trust me to do as I'd promised. Actually I made my will in your favour the day before we were married.'

Frances' eyes widened at this gross misunderstanding of her actions. It was logical, but so untrue. She had wanted to wait for his return among friends, not strangers as his parents would have been, and no thought of using Ian had ever crossed her mind.

'You misjudged me entirely,' she said bitterly.

'I don't think I did. What I saw on the day of my return confirmed my suppositions.'

Frances sprang to her feet and went back to her chair. She faced him across the hearth with indignation in voice and mien.

'You entirely misconstrued what you saw! I thought you'd deserted me for Sam, and so did Ian. He was trying to persuade me to divorce you and marry him. I was about to tell him as gently as I could, because I didn't want to hurt him—he does love me, and his love is sincere—that I could never accept him, when you barged in, and that's the truth, Gray, I swear it! You'd no justification for the bitter things you said to me . . . and to assault me . . .'

He turned his head away and said gruffly:

'I'm sorry for what I did then, Fran. I'd counted so much upon our reunion and when I thought you'd forgotten me, and God knows I could hardly blame you if you had, I saw red. I wanted to hurt you . . . I did hurt you, didn't I?'

'Yes,' she said simply, but she did not mean the physical bruising, but the pain of his distrust.

He looked at her almost humbly. 'For that I would ask you to forgive me. I would like us to part friends.'

'Part?' she echoed blankly.

'It would be best . . . for you. The chivalrous Ian with his sincere love,' an acid note crept into his voice, 'will make you a much better husband than myself. You know by now that I have a savage temper when I'm roused, and recent events have not improved it. You wouldn't find me easy to live with, and you must know too that the man you thought you loved never really existed. Like many another you glamorised me, but the reality is harsh and selfish. It's been dinned in to me how generous you were giving your inheritance to Crawfords, and that shall be paid back to you. I want you to be happy, Fran, and forget me if you can.'

'Which I can never do, and you're talking a load of rubbish. I love you Gray, harsh, selfish, what you will, and I'll never love anyone else. There's no happiness for me without you.'

She looked at him with her heart in her eyes, but there was no response in his still face.

'Lesley tells me you want to go back to England. That's a very good idea . . .'

'That was when I thought you wanted to be free to marry Samantha.'

He exclaimed in horror, 'Good God!'

'Well, it did seem like it at one time,' Frances pointed out. 'But, Gray, there's one person you seem to have forgotten, who needs you even more than I do, and he's your responsibility just as much as mine, though you've tried to ignore him.' Her voice became accusing. 'He could have cost me my life, and you never even thought of what might have occurred. You're so wrapped up in your own woes and vengeances you don't want to see him, but he's there, in the next room, a living entity—your little son.'

A spasm contorted Gray's face, but he said quietly:

'I didn't want to see him because I knew if I did I wouldn't be able to give him up. I've often dreamed of a son, an heir to Crawfords, a boy who would love the sea and boats as I do. But I won't take him away from you, Fran, that wouldn't be fair.'

Frances gave an exasperated sigh.

'My dear man, there's no need to punish yourself to that extent!' she exclaimed. She again dropped on her knees beside him, seizing his hands, those scarred hands that had once been so beautiful, and gazed appealingly into his face.

'Oh, Gray, can't we forget all the ugly things that have happened and start again? You and I and Robbie?'

Then Gray broke. He bowed his head upon their clasped hands, the proud, bitter man who had faced so much disaster with fortitude bent his neck at last. Freeing one hand, Frances gently stroked the fair hair as something like a sob shook his frame.

'Don't, Gray, don't,' she whispered. 'It's all right.'

He lifted his head and she saw his eyes were wet.

'I was so beastly to you.'

'I've forgotten it. I only remember I love you, Gray.'

'If I loved you before I worship you now,' he said humbly.

'Don't be so extravagant,' she chided him gently. 'It's ... out of character ...' She laughed shakily, but her heart swelled with thankfulness and joy, for Gray's eyes gazing into hers were shining with the light of love. 'If I know you, this ... er ... humility won't last long, you'll soon be your old imperious self.'

He smiled wryly. 'I'm afraid you're right, Fran, eating humble pie is not my natural diet, but my pride and arrogance have caused you to suffer. Are you quite sure you wouldn't prefer a gentler mate?'

'Absolutely certain. You are my one and only love.'

'Then since you refuse to be warned, you must take the consequences.'

He scooped her up on to his knees, and encircling her with his arms their lips met in a long satisfying kiss.

Later they stood by the cot in Frances' room in the dim radiance of the nightlight. Sensing something unusual was going on, Robbie opened sleepy eyes. His small legs shot up into the air, displacing the carefully tucked in bedclothes, and he gurgled mischievously.

'That's a favourite trick of his,' Frances told his father. 'Since you're awake, my precious, let Daddy have a look at you.'

She lifted him in her arms, and leaning against

her shoulder, Master Robert Crawford stared at his sire. He waved a chubby arm towards him, and as Gray held out his hand, clutched his finger with a surprisingly strong grip. Gray looked at the tiny digits in wonderment.

'So small, and so perfect!'

'Of course he's perfect, he's our son,' Frances declared. Gray's free arm went round her, drawing her close with the baby between them, and Graham Crawford, the hardbitten cynic, said fervently:

'This is heaven. God make me worthy of you both.'

Harlequin | Plus |

THE FASCINATION OF GLASGOW

Elizabeth Ashton's romantic hero, Gray Crawford, makes his home in Glasgow—and Glasgow, though not a place one would normally consider romantic, is nevertheless a fascinating city. Sprawling on both banks of the River Clyde, Glasgow is an important cosmopolitan seaport and city of contrasts.

Once it was called the Second City—second only to London in size and importance. Originally a center of ecclesiastics and scholars, its enormous medieval cathedral and ancient university, founded in 1450, dominated its activities. Much later, in the eighteenth century, Glasgow's broad streets and elegant squares compared very favorably indeed with the "smelly huddle" that was old Edinburgh town.

But it was Scotland's rich iron and coal fields that helped shape Glasgow's destiny, and during the Industrial Revolution it began to grow into a huge industrial center for ship-building, engineering, chemical plants and distilleries. Now the old and the new, the cultural and industrial blend to make Glasgow one of the most interesting, energetic and productive cities of the north.

Glaswegians, as the Glasgow-born are called, have a reputation for being a realistic, down-to-earth people with a natural argumentativeness. (Is that, you may ask, the real reason for the problems Frances faces with Gray?) But it's said that a sense of humor is their saving grace, and most endearing characteristic.

NEVER BEFORE PUBLISHED

SUPERROMANCE®

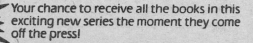

Your chance to receive all the books in this exciting new series the moment they come off the press!

BEST-SELLING SERIES

SUPERROMANCES are the newest best-sellers in the North American romance market.

And no wonder.

EXCITING!

Each SUPERROMANCE contains so much adventure, romance and conflict that it will hold you spellbound until the tumultuous conclusion.

DRAMATIC!

SUPERROMANCE gives you more! More of everything Harlequin is famous for. Spellbinding narratives... captivating heros and heroines...settings that stir the imagination.

1981 brings you...

2 SUPERROMANCES novels every other month.

Each volume contains more than 380 pages of exciting romance reading.

Don't miss this opportunity!

Complete and mail the Subscription Reservation Coupon on the following page TODAY!